THE TEX MURDERS

A

GINGER O'LEARY MYSTERY

BY

CHRIS H. WONDOLOSKI

Chris Wondoloski

Copyright © 2019 Christopher H. Wondoloski
All rights reserved

Cover photograph courtesy of Gene Kemp and The North Adams Historical Society
Copyright © 2019

THE TEXTILE MILL MURDERS is a work of historical fiction. Any names, characters, places, and incidents are either a product of the author's imagination or are used fictitiously. Any resemblance to actual persons, living or dead, business establishments, events or locales is entirely coincidental.

The Textile Mill Murders begins on a sunny October day in 1866 when Ginger O'Leary is convinced by her new husband, CJ Mulcahy, Esq., to play hooky from her studies for the Massachusetts Bar. CJ's plan is to pick up a picnic lunch at the Old Black Tavern and head to the top of Witt's ledge for a bit of supping, dining, and canoodling.

However, as the pair approach their destination, they are confronted by a near-sighted young constable who beckons them to stop. Once CJ identifies himself, the young constable reports to his former sergeant that the body of a young woman had been found earlier that morning at the cliff's base, dead of an apparent suicide. Shocked and curious, CJ and Ginger proceed to the scene and find Ginger's father, constable Captain Charles O'Leary, ranting at sergeant Elisha Smart over the whereabouts of Doc Briggs. "If I find out he's gone off on one o' his benders, or was in an all-night poker game at Dutchy's and can't get his arse outa' bed..."

Nearby and standing alone, they also notice Fr. Charles Lynch, despondent and weeping over the tarp-covered lump of ground that was Shayleigh Grogan. Sensing the prying eyes of onlookers, Ginger and CJ invite the good father for a walk. When he chooses to go to the top of Witt's ledge in order to, "… bask a while in God's good sunshine." Ginger becomes concerned because she is one of the dark ones, a keeper of An Dara Sealladh. If Shayleigh Grogan's despairing spirit were to contact her, Ginger could end up a partner in death beside her.

However, the afternoon atop the cliff passes without incident. And upon their return to the bottom, curiosity causes Ginger to examine the now empty spot where Shayleigh had landed. Hardly any blood. No wonder Shayleigh's spirit was silent. She didn't jump from Witt's ledge. Long before, she was tossed from the cliff like a sack of garbage, Shayleigh Grogan was murdered!

Also by Chris H. Wondoloski

The Hoosac Tunnel Murders

I'd like to acknowledge the creative assistance and patience of my good friends Patricia Prenguber, Justyna Carlson, and Gene Carlson and The North Adams Historical Society

My entire family, and the love of my life, Sharon Mulcahy Wondoloski

for Gail O'Brien

Chapter 1
October 1866

The break which initiated the process of solving *The Hoosac Tunnel Murders* cropped up as the bleakness of late winter was replaced by the radiance of spring. In like manner, the pall that had hung over the village of North Adams and the O'Leary family during those dark months was replaced by exhilaration.

Justice had prevailed.

The flawed and tormented souls of Ned Brinkman and Billy Nash, which had been so coldly and mercilessly torn asunder, now had company in Hell. One by one, their murderer, as well as the men who had ordered this despicable act, paid for their treachery with their own lives.

And I, for one, am extremely proud of my part in helping these men on their way.

My name is Virginia O'Leary Mulcahy. My friends and family call me Ginger. Others call me ... well, witch is among the kinder monikers. While it is true I'm one of the dark ones, I'm not a witch. And I certainly don't worship the devil. What I am is a very tall, flaming haired Celtic colleen with buttermilk skin and eyes the color of the Irish countryside. Catholic to my bones, I have simply inherited a gift handed down in our family from the ancient time of the druids.

I often see things ... things that *will* happen, or touch things and explain what *has* happened. I can even force people to confront the evil they have hidden away within themselves. However, this power is fraught with peril. While manipulating another person's mind or awakening a conscience long ago suppressed might unnerve the guilty; it can also destroy the innocent, me included. Visions of murder and death invade and drain me, leaving me vulnerable to the evil souls I encounter who reach out and clutch for mine. You see, it's at that moment of contact, *they* know that *I* know; our souls are laid bare to one another, and only guile and determination will determine the victor.

Doesn't sound like much of a gift, does it? At times it isn't. Stewardship of the second sight, or An Dara Sealladh, can be more of a burden than a gift. Unless used to help others, it is little more than a parlor trick ... a most dangerous curiosity.

But it *is* my destiny, so I accept it and embrace it.

However, prudent use of An Dara Sealladh demands wisdom of the ages, a deep understanding of the human condition and complete knowledge of the law. And that's a tall order for someone barely twenty. Someone like me.

So, while there is no school of the second sight I can attend, I thankfully *do* have help in these three areas.

Guidance in the first has come to me in the form of my baal or spirit guide, whom I strongly suspect is my own grandmother Saorla. While alive, she too possessed the second sight and was revered by all of County Cork for her wisdom and ability to find the truth. Although she crossed over long before my birth, she knew that someday I would come to be; and so, her spirit continues to feel responsible for me. One time, during the darkest hours of this past year, she saved me from succumbing to the temptation of using divination for personal gain. Her questions probed my motives, forcing me to choose what I stood for and who I was. On another, she guided me toward trapping two murderous conspirators into convicting themselves.

For counsel on the second I have m' Da, Captain Charles James O'Leary, chief officer of the North Adams Constabulary and Samuel N. Briggs, M.D. whose ostensible respectability belies a nature which thoroughly enjoys operating in the seamy gutter world of North Adams, barely one step ahead of Captain O'Leary's attention. Together, they've taught me about the relative nature of people and of justice. Absolute good exists only in Heaven, absolute evil in Hell. So, if it's concrete answers you're after, you'll unfortunately need to die. The rest of us are left to swing between the extremes, hung by our personal pendulums, doing the best we can.

And as for the third ... ah, the third ... that's why I'm sitting, on this beautiful October afternoon, in the library of the newest law firm in North Adams, *Colgrove and Mulcahy* ... staring at this law book ... *not* seeing, let alone comprehending, the pages which lay before me. And so, tempted by the humid warmth of this early autumn afternoon, I find myself lapsing into daydreams of the Saturday morning this past June when I pledged my troth to the love of my life, Conal John Mulcahy. And he to me.

On that glorious late spring morning, the sun was on its odyssey in pursuit of the summer solstice rather than retreating from it; and the mountains were donning verdant cloaks rather than abandoning them for the fiery hues of early autumn.

So, here I was, lost in the revelry of that fairy tale when the sudden massaging of my shoulders from behind dragged me back to the here and now.

"Penny for your thoughts?"

"CJ! How did you ever get your law degree? Case law is *so* boring and locked up by precedent. Outcomes often defy logic. It seems that winning a case depends on discovering some obscure ruling the other side has overlooked and nothing at all to do with fairness or justice. It's all a game isn't it, CJ ... a bloody game with a person's liberty or property at stake. I hate it, CJ! I hate it "

CJ released his grip on my shoulders, took a seat facing me and held my hands in his.

"Ginger, case law is like learning your times tables. It gives you a solid basis upon which you build to solve problems. Real court is still based upon using common sense to achieve justice. None of the judges I know tolerate the gamesmanship of employing obscure precedents. In the judge's eyes any prosecutor or defense attorney who tries it weakens his argument. Case Law is also like history, Ginger. Understanding mistakes of the past prevent us from repeating them. Likewise, the logic of success demonstrates what will work."

At that CJ rose from his chair and standing before me laughed,

"Now that I've parroted most of the lecture I was given my very first day of class at Albany Law School, let me confess that Professor Irving Quinn Tanguay's fascination with the subject has always escaped me as well."

And calling over his shoulder as he walked out of the library Conal continued,

"Anyhow, School's out, Virginia. Let's flee this salt mine!"

Looking after his receding figure I was at first uncertain CJ was indeed serious. But when he paused at the doorway and flashed his trademark impish grin, I was convinced, and offered in my very best Irish brogue,

"So, Conal John, 'tis hooky we'll be playin' this afternoon. What'll Jeremiah say?"

At that CJ reversed his course and pulled me from my chair until I rose to my full height. Forced to look up at me from some three inches below, Conal taunted,

"Since when are you afraid of Jeremiah?"

Afraid of Jeremiah? Never!

Jeremiah Colgrove III is not only my boss and sponsor to the Massachusetts Bar, he has been my best friend since we first met in grammar school. Even then both of us towered over our age mates, and more than any of the others we seemed to revel in the world of thoughts and ideas. Our precocious thirst for knowledge and insufferable need to understand the why of everything both ostracized us from our peers and drove our teachers around the bend.

When Jeremiah went on to high school at Drury Academy and society relegated me to the family dairy farm to learn homemaking, the anger we both felt prevented either of us from accepting it. Jeremiah "procured" textbooks for me which I promptly devoured, and we met every afternoon we could to discuss the lessons of the week. Jeremiah preferred coming to our dairy farm at the foot of the Hoosac Mountains, and I the Colgrove manse on Church Street in the heart of the village. Jeremiah, because he loved Ma's cooking, and I to get off the damned mountain for even a little while.

When Jeremiah graduated from Drury Academy and headed off to Harvard Law School, my sense of loss and abandonment spiraled downward by the day. There was a hole in the pit of my gut. I missed my friend and I thirsted for the life he was leading. What a world college must be!

And yes, I was jealous.

However, it couldn't have been more than a couple of weeks before Da began bringing home packages of books. The return address on the wrapper always read Harvard, nothing else.

Jeremiah!

Even today, the memory of that first delivery still warms my heart. Straight away, I began immersing myself in the classics: Philosophy, Euclidean mathematics, Greek mythology, Shakespeare, and on and on.

My angel hath delivered me.

Through the years the advantages and limitations of Victorian society drove us to forge a bond of mutual respect and reciprocal love. Alas, as we matured it was destined to never become more than that. From our earliest days our most placid exchanges of ideas were wont to explode into tirades of expository logic few could follow, and into which only the most-foolhardy attempted to intervene. The facts were, the worlds in which our characters incubated were so vastly different we viewed life from entirely different perspectives.

Jeremiah unconsciously used and manipulated people around him in a manner he may have considered benign, but I often considered self-serving. Growing up surrounded by servants and people of the village who bowed to the power and influence of his parents, Jeremiah rarely heard the word no. No one was immune from his perpetual gamesmanship, not even me. And that was when sparks would fly! I greatly resented Jeremiah's attitude because he *knew* I was more than his intellectual equal. Furthermore, it was he himself who had made me privy to the game he so successfully played with others. How could I not be insulted?

And "no" was definitely in my vocabulary.

But the disarming charm and supreme confidence with which Jeremiah navigated through society also completely endeared him to me. These were exactly the qualities I lacked. You see, I'm brash and can sometimes even be crude, given to impetuous actions that have gotten me into more than a little trouble, on more than one occasion. But unlike Jeremiah, any expressions of arrogance I displayed were more to cover self-doubt than due to a sense of entitlement or superiority.

But not in this case!

"You're right, CJ. It's Emancipation Day. Let's go!"

Chapter 2
The Best Laid Plans …

As CJ and I made our escape out the back door to the horse stable, we found Hessie, my gray Appaloosa mare, all saddled and calmly waiting at the hitching post. One of CJ's most endearing qualities was that he not only understood my nature, he accepted it. Conal knew there'd be no horse and buggy on this day … or just about any day. Day dress or jodhpurs, it made little difference. I ride.

But what of CJ's charcoal three-year old, Killian? When we poked our heads in the stable, we found Jimmy the stableman vainly attempting to adequately tighten the saddle's cinch strap as Killian huffed, puffed and arrogantly stomped around.

"Theweet! Killian, boy," CJ commanded.

That horse so immediately ceased resistance that the heavily sweating stableman ran into Killian's left haunch only to be bumped off by one final shift of the horse's hip. When Jimmy turned to face us, a mixture of consternation and exasperation covered his face, but he said nothing. I couldn't help smiling to myself because the only one huffing and puffing now was Jimmy.

Cinch strap finally secured; Jimmy anxiously turned the reins over to CJ. As he did, the pat he delivered to the horse's haunch seemed to have a little extra zest behind it. The completely oblivious Killian nuzzled CJ's side for a reward. In *his* mind he was a good boy because he answered CJ's command. And sure enough, CJ opened his palm and offered Killian the carrot he knew CJ carried in his jacket pocket. Then CJ soothed the stableman's consternation with a silver dollar from his other pocket while sheepishly offering a sincere,

"Thank you, Mr. Tomaselli."

Finally mounted, we passed from the stable area, through the alleyway between the opulent Adams National Bank Building to our left and the brand new Colgrove Building, home of *Colgrove and Mulcahy*. Now on Main Street, we turned left, and found I could hold my sarcasm no longer.

"There's no question, Conal, your indulgence of that horse's behavior certainly ensures no one will ever steal him."

CJ, seemingly as oblivious as his damned horse, and quite pleased with himself, beamed. Totally exasperated, I blurted,

"Of course, when word gets around, you're also guaranteeing you'll always saddle your own horse."

CJ simply reached over, patted Killian on the shoulder and smiled,

"I sent a message to the Old Black Tavern a while ago. Our picnic lunch is waiting. You want to give advice, or do you want to spend the afternoon up on Witt's ledge supping, dining and canoodling with the love of your life?"

I simply shook my head and sighed. The answer was obvious, especially since CJ loved that horse almost as much as he loved me … and was actually proud that Killian acceded to no man except him.

The distance to the Old Black Tavern was only two blocks west and on the south side of Main Street. First built in the late 1700's, it occupied the east corner of State Street and Main and was a rickety wooden holdout against the brick and granite progress overtaking the rest of downstreet North Adams. The black paint which gave the inn its name had long since peeled away leaving the inn's clapboards to appear as dried-out, graying bones.

Upon entering the tavern and closing the door behind us, CJ and I were confronted by an eerie twilight emanating though the small, grime-covered windows. The clamor of Main Street was shut out so abruptly the quiet was deafening. Once our eyes and ears adjusted to this world apart, we approached the bar to collect our picnic lunch. Only inches above my head, I could easily reach up and touch the rough-hewn beams which prevented the ceiling from collapsing on our heads. The floorboards squeaked with age as they yielded to our weight and oozed the aroma of countless years of spilled beer and expelled bodily fluids. Not one person turned to greet us. Physically broken down and discarded by life or addicted to drink, these weekday patrons of the Old Black Tavern had little reason to be friendly.

But the barman did.

"Ahhhh, 'afternoon, Sergeant Mulcahy." And nodding his head toward me ... "Missus."

"Cookie work his usual magic for us, Gus?"

"Of course, sir. Hasn't changed things up in nigh on forty years now, has he?"

At that we all shared a hearty chuckle. The Old Black Tavern might have been a broken-down hole in the wall, but when it came to food ... oh the food ... simply the best! For hearty, everyday fare not even the vaunted Wilson House, directly across the way on Main Street, stacked up. The joke shared throughout the village spake that it was Cookie's kitchen hygiene, or lack of it … as well as the decades-long buildup of bacon grease on every vessel and utensil used in the kitchen that was responsible.

"Here you are, sir, all packed in saddlebags as you asked."

Then Gus bent forward over the bar and added conspiratorially, "I'd handle 'em careful, sir. Got a bit of a liquid surprise for you and the missus in there. Don't go shakin' 'em, if you get my drift, sir."

I too leaned forward, gave Gus a quick peck on the top of his balding head and said,

"Gus, you're a peach."

Very pleased with himself, Gus was still laughing out loud as we closed the door behind us. One of the things I liked best about the Old Black Tavern was that it was one of the few places left in the village where being kissed by a witch made a man laugh instead of running to find the nearest church and seek out his pastor.

As soon as we remounted, our destination appeared in the distance above us, less than a half-mile down State

Street to the south. Witt's ledge was an outcropping at the base of the foothills of the Mt. Greylock range so steep and so tall that it was forever unclaimed by soil-cover or vegetation of any kind. It's also why two stone masons, Ivory and Pliny Witt purchased it in the 1850's, dug out a short road connecting it to State Street, and posted a sign stating that *Witt's Ledge Lime-Marble Quarry* was open for business.

However, the Witts were primarily stone masons and satisfied to cleave off only what was needed to provide limestone for the facade of some new building on Main Street or marble for the fireplace fronts and mantles of the Church Street mansions. Their materials and workmanship beyond rival, Ivory and Pliny were very selective about the few contracts they accepted each year and still made a fine living.

This of course, meant that most of the time few workmen were around the quarry. So, those hearty enough to follow the path quarrymen used to reach the cliff at the top of the ledge were treated to not only solitude, but also a beautiful panoramic view of nearly the entire village. That's why CJ had chosen it for this afternoon's supping, dining ... and maybe just a bit of canoodling. And why I couldn't wait to get there!

However, after we passed State Street Rail Depot, crossed the short bridge which carried us over the Hoosic River, and urged our horses up the hill to take the unpaved carriageway euphemistically named Witt Avenue, we found our progress abruptly halted by a young constable. Raising his arm in the air, he fixed us with the sternest scowl his callow expression could offer and said,

"Hold on right there, folks. Nuthin' but trouble up ahead. Gotta' stop yuz' right here!"

When CJ called out to him, "Constable Cowlin, what sort of trouble are we talking about, son?" The young constable proved to be more than slightly near-sighted as he squinted, lowered his arm, and returned,

"Sergeant Mulcahy? S'that 'chu, sir?"

CJ leaned over as he whispered to me, "First day on the job I told Cowlin to get himself a pair of glasses before he walked into a door. Can hardly see past the tip of his nose."

I had to work hard to conceal a laugh as CJ answered,

"How are those specs coming, son?"

Cowlin flushed as he approached us and sheepishly nodded greetings to me,

"Aw, sir, you know how 'tiz. Can you 'magine how them gutter snipes'd treat me wearin' a pair of windows on my nose? An' since you got yurself married to Miss Virginia here, and left the force 'n all ...Well, I guess I forgot, sir."

CJ shook his head and smiled,

"Well you don't have any knots on your head, so I guess you haven't walked into any doors yet."

Constable Cowlin flushed and gave a quick, uneasy chuckle. He didn't seem to know whether to hold his ground or flee, so instead he proceeded to report. It didn't matter that CJ was no longer a constable sergeant, he was the young man's first superior officer and that still counted for something.

"Mr. Pliny Witt, proprietor of Witt's Quarry paid a call to the station at seven-thirty this mornin' and talked to Sergeant Smart. Said when he got to work, he found a dead woman, no more 'n seventeen-eighteen, at the bottom of the ledge. Appeared to him she either fell or jumped sometime last night."

The joking was immediately over, the smiles were gone. A young woman had been snatched from our midst long, long before her time. CJ and I looked at each other, the unspoken questions obvious...Who...and why?

Chapter 3
Hidden Potential/Missed Potential

As we approached the scene of the young woman's demise it became quite evident that despite the best efforts of constable Cowlin, word had spread among folks living nearby. Several women still wearing household aprons congregated along the outskirts of the quarry. Some hugged themselves and looked down, examining the ground at their feet. Others turned away but gazed into the sky, the silent movement of their lips a telltale sign of the prayers they offered. The men maneuvered to get as close to the scene as the cordon of constables would allow. Shielding their eyes from the early afternoon sun with one hand and pointing up nearly two hundred feet to the top of Witt's ledge with the other, more than a few of the men quietly murmured to their friends the version of events they had reconstructed. Some folks were leaving, while others continued to appear through the surrounding overgrowth. It wouldn't be long before the young woman's death would be the talk of the village.

Exchanging nods with the first perimeter constable we encountered, CJ and I crossed the rope cordon, but hadn't gone far before we drew next to a very preoccupied, solitary figure. Dressed entirely in black and slightly taller than CJ, this powerfully built man had fixed his gaze upon the blanket covering a lump of ground some twenty or thirty feet away and was completely unaware of our presence.

"Father, Father Lynch ..."

I had hardly uttered his name when our young pastor returned to reality with a pronounced start and turned to face us. Tears were streaming down his cheeks and only after taking a collecting deep breath or two did he sob,

"Virginia Daelyn ... Conal John ... she was one o' the flock. One o' mine. So young, so pure. She had no one ... no one!" Then the good father trailed off, "And she died such a ... such a terrible lonely death."

CJ and I looked at each other, touched by the humanity Father Lynch had revealed to us. But what comfort could we offer within eyesight of so many unequipped to see him as just a man? People who required an icon of strength as the head of their families expected ... no ... they required, no less in the pastor of their church.

So, I settled for casually looping my arm through his and said,

"Father, we're so very sorry. D'ya' think we might take a stroll and have a chat about what happened?"

With his free hand, Father Lynch reached across, patted my intertwined arm, and said,

"Grand idea, Virginia, just grand. What say we all head on up t' the top o' the ledge and bask a while in God's good sunshine?"

Father's choice of venue for our chat was both brilliant ... and not. While it seemed to be a fitting place to discuss what may have driven the young woman lying dead only a few feet away to commit such a disconsolate act, it might also harbor vestiges of her restless soul. If that were the case, there was no telling the effect she would have on me.

After all, just last year the murdered and vengeful spirits of Ned Brinkman and Billy Nash had taken complete control of my body, while my being was transported through time to a different place. The result of that experience *did* provide the first real clue as to who was responsible for the tragedy in the Hoosac Tunnel, but it also nearly destroyed my life-long friendship with Jeremiah Colgrove.

Today, it wasn't social embarrassment or the loss of a friend I was concerned about. It was entirely conceivable that a visit so near to the cliff's edge might result in my joining the young woman in death at the bottom.

Nevertheless, off we went. Unfortunately, in doing so we needed to get by my very agitated father, Constable Captain Charles James O'Leary, chief officer of the North Adams Constabulary. Pacing back and forth, all six feet, fourteen stone of the man subordinates called "the bear" bellowed at CJ's thunderstruck replacement, Sergeant Elisha Smart. As we walked by, I doubt Da even noticed the three of us. But Sergeant Smart did. And all he managed was a curt nod and a tortured smile. It was clear that at that moment he longed for his nice quiet desk at the constable station and CJ's return to duty.

"Where the hell is Doctor Briggs!" Da roared. We've been waitin' hours now for his sorry arse t' show. If I find out he's gone off on one o' his benders, or was in an all-night poker game at Dutchy's and can't get his arse out' bed..."

Thankfully, once we had run the gauntlet, the sound of Da's bellowing faded a bit more with every step we took and was replaced by the sound of breezes rustling the leaves of the trees. The path we followed to the top of the ledge was well-worn and easy to follow. Quarry workers used it so they could secure purchase for the ropes from which they dangled to examine the rock face. On weekends young couples used it to reach the gently sloping field which abruptly terminated at the cliff's edge and provided a spectacular view of the village center. Today, the kind of privacy CJ and I hoped for had been refocused as a mission allowing his riv'rence to safely release his anguish and grief to sympathetic ears.

However, once we reached the top, Father Lynch seemed recomposed by the cool, gentle breezes and warm October sun. He fearlessly proceeded to the cliff's edge. Locking his hands behind his back, Father Lynch stood transfixed, rocking back and forth from toe to heel, and proclaimed to no one particular,

"Could any day be lovelier?"

Shocked, I looked at CJ, cocked my head askew, and raised an eyebrow. I don't know what I expected. I guess I thought Father Lynch would immediately open his soul and spew its contents to CJ and me. Screams of anger. Tears of anguish. Something. Anything. But not this!

After all, he *had* spent Sunday evenings at the O'Leary family homestead at least once a month since I was a child. Ma's feasts sated him. More than a few three finger jars of John Jameson's elixir of the gods pickled him. And the family hearth melted his guard. I'd observed Da and Father Lynch open up to one another about village and parish problems as to no one else. Sharing their frustrations and anger always proved cathartic; working out potential solutions, restorative. I knew Father Lynch's strengths and weaknesses. I knew his moods. So, the reaction to this young woman's death playing out before me was completely out of character and totally opposite the abject sorrow the good Father displayed not ten minutes ago.

Parishioners of St. Francis had died tragic deaths before. More often than not they had been young as well. Not long ago, a man barely in his twenties had been killed by his own freight wagon. As he unloaded his delivery, the horse team became startled by a loud noise. When he rushed to prevent a runaway by grabbing the reins, the young man slipped under the wheels and was crushed. On another occasion, a young mother, her child, and their home were consumed in flames caused by a kitchen grease fire. Neither of these had resulted in anything from Father Lynch but a guise of strength which assisted the families to maintain their faith in God and heaven. But before me stood not that man of strength and faith. Instead, CJ and I beheld a tortured soul who sought to hide the damnable pain which sickened his heart by projecting a façade of denial.

While I stood lost in puzzlement of what to do next, it was CJ who took control by whispering to me,

"I've seen this before. After a battle, it wasn't at'all unusual for one of my soldiers to be standing in the middle of blood and gore, and oblivious to his surroundings, comment about some vision of beauty his mind had chosen to see instead. When that happens there's nothing helpful you can say. So, if we're patient, provide comfort and just listen, the good father will talk *himself* back to reality. Trust me, it will be enough."

CJ then gave my hand a quick squeeze, "But, be prepared. *How* he comes back to us may be quite..."

I nodded curt affirmation to Conal that I understood. CJ took a deep breath and called out, projecting this time so father could hear,

"Father, why not come on back here and take a load off? Virginia and I have brought along a wonderful picnic lunch here ..."

Nothing.

"Plenty, if you care to join us ..."

Again, nothing.

"It's from the Old Black Tavern ..."

Father Lynch turned and smiled.

CJ cocked his head at the two amber bottles he held up and pointed them invitingly toward father,

"Thirsty?"

That did it. When Father approached and parked himself side-saddle to join us, I couldn't help but smile to myself.

I know CJ told me to allow Father Lynch to talk his way out of it, but can it hurt to prime the pump a bit? Here goes...

"I never realized before, your riv'rence, but that cassock of yours presents the same problems as my day dress."

"That it does, Virginia," Father Lynch chuckled. "Livin' in this village, I've often wished I was allowed t' wear trousers and boots every day, I can tell ya'."

Father grinned broadly while shaking his head back and forth, seeming to recall a happy scene, and remarked, "Last fall I went up t' the Burk farm t' lend Dan a hand cuttin' and stackin' cord wood for the coming winter. By the time I arrived, I was so eager t' get at it I shed the damned cassock right over m' head without so much as a thought. Well, it looked to me that Mrs. Burk would go t' faintin'! Was dressed exactly as Dan, but it was too much for the precious woman."

Father looked pensive for just a moment and smiled, "I wonder what the good woman thought I wore underneath?"

Then, the light left his eyes for a moment as he finished, "Sometimes I think parishioners actually believe priests are born in cassocks and Roman collars."

CJ uncorked a beer bottle with a pop and a fizz, handed it to Father Lynch and remarked, "Well I do have to tell you, Father, you are a most unusual pastor. Gathering hay, planting fields, splitting and stacking cord wood ... You love to toil and sweat, sir."

Very good, Conal. I primed the pump. You work the handle a bit. Let's get the water flowing.

Unfazed by CJ's bait, Father paused for what seemed a very long time. In the meantime, CJ distributed bottles of beer to both of us. He and I avoided father's eyes as we clinked our bottles together, took deep draughts, and feigned lack of concern at his lack of response.

For the rest of our lunch it seemed there would *be* none.

As time dragged on, I found myself nervously nibbling around the edges of a chicken leg. However, oblivious to the mounting tension I sensed, CJ devoured his... and a bowl of Cookie's famous apple cider vinegar and sugar dressed coleslaw as well.

Father Lynch contented himself with accepting the second pint of beer CJ offered to him. However, after one or two short pulls on the spout, he placed the bottle on the ground and set to ripping out thatches of grass and tossing them to the wind.

In response, CJ rolled over onto his back, cradled both of his hands behind his head and absently gazed out at the village skyline.

I, on the other hand, chewed the inside of my cheek raw in an effort to suppress a scream.

Patience, girl ... patience.

My heart beat faster by the minute and my ears began to ring. I struggled to maintain an outward calm but found myself fidgeting and picking at pills in the fabric of my day dress.

Just when I thought I would burst Father Lynch abruptly rose to a sitting position and crossed his legs. I just couldn't help myself. I peeked. And then I giggled,

"I'm so sorry, your riv'rence, I just had to see if you did, indeed, have on trousers under that cassock."

The harmony created by the laughs of my contralto, CJ's baritone and Father Lynch's tenor resonated so loudly they startled nearby birds into giving up their perches and flying away.

Chapter 4
A Lovely Day

"Virginia O'Leary Mulcahy!" CJ burst out, aghast with false abashment.

The resultant new round of laughs only served to further punctuate the afternoon's unease and replace it with a relaxed air, albeit temporarily.

"Tis fine, Conal, 'tis fine. I guess the horrible death of ... let's do her the honor of calling her by her name ... Shayleigh, Shayleigh Grogan, brought to a head many conflicting feelings of m' own. Almost from the first day she arrived here from Ireland, Shayleigh confided to me that she was picked as her family's best hope for the future. On the verge of starvation, they scrounged t' fund her passage to America. She fought against leavin' till the day her father placed her on the ship bound for America."

"The plan was for Shayleigh t' settle here and send money back as soon as she could. But she found she couldn't, and probably never would be able to. A large portion of what little money Shayleigh earned in the textile mill was gone as soon as she received it. Between the rent she paid for the company-owned apartment she shared with three other girls, and the food she bought at the company store, her future was bleak. Her only hope t' make extra money was to become very good at piece work and produce more than expected. But, Shayleigh was a Connemara farm girl who was clumsy and confused around machinery and found it difficult t' even keep up."

"There was little comfort to be gotten from the other girls she lived with either because they came and went almost as soon as she learned their names. Some chose life on the streets; others were lucky enough t' marry. Neither of these choices seemed likely for Shayleigh since the gift of beauty hadn't been visited upon her. So, circumstances beyond her control sentenced her t' remain working in the mill and livin' in the row house. In the end she had nothin'. And Shayleigh may have lived in a world surrounded by people, but she was still alone."

At that, Fr. Lynch exhaled a long, downhearted sigh and said:

"I suppose the despair and loneliness Shayleigh felt drove her to this. And for that I am profoundly sad."

Father then paused and stole a furtive glance at both of us before stunning me so completely I felt disoriented.

"When I first identified her body for your father this mornin', I saw not only *Shayleigh's* face, but I also saw m' own."

"You see, in m' quietest hours I'm haunted by guilt, as well, for bein' the one chosen. The one elevated above m' brothers and sister, for reasons I never understood. I never asked for it. I never wanted it. And believe me when I tell ya', I felt no divine intervention in my vocation ... only m' Ma's."

"I came of age at just the time England's Penal laws were bein' relaxed after strangling us for nearly two centuries. Irish seminaries were re-opening and it was the duty of every family in Ireland to commit a son t' the priesthood. It's for that reason I was sent t' St. Patrick's College in Carlow rather than workin' the family fields of Ballyjamesduff." I was little more than a boy and a choice was never offered ...

His riv'rence then took a final, deep draught from his beer bottle, rolled the empty along the ground to CJ, and finished,

"So, you're quite right, Conal. There *have* been more than a few days when I'd rather split wood than say Mass. All *I* ever wanted was t' give honor to the deity by working the land so hard each day that my hands bled ...

and by havin' a family of m' own. It's probably why I'm so drawn to pitchin' in any time I can to help the young families of the parish. Sittin' alone in the rectory only stirs up similar feelings as must've driven Shayleigh t' end her pain. It's definitely why seein' her broken body not only saddens me so ... it terrifies me."

Whoa! Despair? Loneliness? St. Francis has over two thousand parishioners! Fr. Lynch always seems so happy ... so involved ... How ...?

How, indeed! Well, CJ warned you. When the good Father chose to open up it could shock you ... and you cut him off ... you thought you knew. Well, did ya' girl?

Father Lynch suddenly rose, turned toward the cliff of Witt's ledge and began walking toward the edge. I tried to call out to him, but CJ seized my arm and shook his head in such a definite manner I stopped. Nevertheless, I attempted to shrug him off and rise, but his grip only tightened to the point of hurting me. When I turned back again to protest, I was met this time by the tortured countenance I'd only seen my dearest love display once before. It was last year ... that day in the "bloody pit."

And then I knew. CJ had not only been talking about war and its effect on his men; he was talking also about *himself*. He had been where Father Lynch was now. He understood in a way I could not. So, I surrendered.

"Ginger, please," CJ emphatically whispered. "This is it. This is *his* moment. *He* needs to resolve this for himself. It's between him and God right now."

Then CJ smiled that smile; that combination of sadness and joy which had caused me to fall so in love with him. That smile of a man who had been to hell but demanded release.

Would I ever understand?

We both watched Father reach the edge, but he went no farther. He stood as he had when we first arrived. Hands clasped behind his back, he rocked … toe to heel … heel to toe … toe to heel …

We waited for what seemed an eternity but were only a few minutes. Then, Father Charles Lynch called out once again to no one in particular,

"Could any day be lovelier?"

But this time when he turned to face us, there was no wistful, vacant stare. There was only resolve.

"Thank you for the most wonderful picnic, my friends. But it's time we were back. There's much work t' do!"

Chapter 5
Among the Rocks

The walk down from the top of Witt's ledge was thankfully quiet. No one spoke as we picked our way through the path which always seemed steeper in this direction. It gave each of us time to reflect upon what had transpired over the past hour and a half. It also gave me time to brood over what had not. Shayleigh Grogan's spirit hadn't approached me in any form. The sun never darkened, my being hadn't been engulfed by her shade, nor was I drawn to the precarious edge of the cliff. I hadn't even experienced a sense of despondent sorrow or anguish ... Nothing.

So why da' ya' think that is?

Indeed! Why hadn't she? I couldn't help but feel ... Disappointed? Disregarded?

Knock it, Ginger! Have ya' learned nothing? It'isn't about you ... Never is. T'is about Shayleigh. Now think!

I was still pondering an answer to that question when we reached the bottom. No din of whispering observers sharing their versions of events greeted us. No bellowing Captain O'Leary. No browbeaten and withered Sergeant Smart. No stogie chomping Doctor Briggs ... Nobody... No ...body. We were alone.

Remarkably, there was no apparent evidence anything had occurred here at all! Without saying a word, the three of us approached the spot where we believed Shayleigh Grogan's body had come to rest. I felt like the worst kind of voyeur because of the strange affinity I felt to ogle. No spirit was responsible, only my morbid curiosity. Where exactly did her body come to rest? I certainly couldn't tell from where we were.

Then Father Lynch pointed to a spot just a few feet to our right and said,

"T'is there. I remember that collection o' rocks from when I administered Extreme Unction and conditional absolution to Miss Grogan earlier this mornin'."

When CJ and I snapped our heads around exchanging shocked and questioning expressions, Father Lynch smiled but could only whisper,

"I'm fully aware that some priests are absolutists and view suicide as an unpardonable sin against God. But can any of us know for certain what was in Shayleigh's heart when she tumbled off that cliff? I am but a man ... an agent of God. In my mind and heart she deserved the sacraments which would assist her t' face the judgement only the deity has the right to make."

Ach, Father Charles Lynch, but aren't ya' the sweetest man in the whole world. If there's any chance at'all for Shayleigh to enter heaven, you'll see to it.

Together we took the last couple of steps. Still, it wasn't until we were right on top of the place Father Lynch had pointed out that we were able to see any evidence of the horrible event. There were a few blood smudges on the flat rocks and three or four small deep purple clots which had puddled between the sharp ones. Nothing else.

Think, Ginger, think!

Before I had a chance to proffer my suspicions, CJ blurted,

"My, God, she was already dead when she landed!"

Feeling the dim-wit for not arriving at the same conclusion, I attempted to recoup my honor by nodding in agreement and emphatically adding the obvious,

"And she didn't die here."

There wasn't more than a moment's pause before a thoroughly stunned Father Lynch positively exploded,

"What?"

Then he bent at the knees, reached out and passed his open palm over the area as if searching for contradictory evidence. He even moved a few of the smaller rocks to see if by some chance more blood had dripped underneath them. Finally, satisfied there was none, Father quietly responded with a drawn out and melodic lilt which conveyed the surprise and anger we all felt.

"Well ... I'll ... be ... damned!"

Suddenly, the persona of Conal J. Mulcahy Esq. was gone and a completely enraged constable sergeant CJ Mulcahy emerged from hibernation.

"We need to find the Captain and Doctor Briggs. I'm not sure what *did* happen, but I do know this ... Shayleigh Grogan did not commit suicide. Let's go!"

Thank God, my man is back! CJ, m' love, I've missed ya'.

And I'm back... We're back! And we have a murder to solve.

Chapter 6
Get On With It!

Killian, who had been calmly grazing with Hessie, and Father Lynch's carriage horse sensed CJ's sudden change in demeanor as he approached, snorted and fought restraint as soon as CJ mounted. The muscles of his powerful haunches standing proud, he stomped back and forth, begging for the command to go. Struggling to maintain control, CJ managed to call down something neither I nor Father Lynch was able to discern, so I returned,

"For heaven's sake, go, CJ! We'll catch up."

I didn't need to tell him twice either. Released, Killian immediately reared up, bolted to a gallop and they were gone in a cloud of dust.

Thankfully, our destination from Witt's Quarry was less than a half-mile down Witt Avenue, across State Street, by the rail depot, and due east up the Summer Street knoll to Village Hall and Constable Station. While I wanted more than anything to mount up and challenge the lads, I thought better of it. So, after mounting Hessie I prepared to accompany the equally anxious Father Lynch who had already hopped up onto his carriage.

However, I'd forgotten, *this* good father was no priss. He snapped the reins in a skilled way, turning them into a two-pronged whip. Crack! His carriage horse's haunches were spanked and off it bolted with the good father holding on for dear life as Hessie and I struggled to keep up.

Of this I was sure; our departure may not have been as impressive as CJ and Killian's, but we trailed a big cloud of dust behind, nonetheless!

We arrived no more than a minute or two after CJ. Father jumped off before his carriage came to rest, while I dismounted only a bit less perilously. Together we headed down the outside stairs leading to the basement of Village Hall, and the home of the North Adams Constabulary. The outside door was vibrating from being violently thrown open against the station's granite wall and still swinging to and fro from the pain. I smiled when I heard the raised, but familiar voices.

"Where's the girl's body? You didn't send her off to the Adams brothers yet did you?"

Father Lynch and I entered just as CJ finished his question. An ignored but smiling Sergeant Smart sat at his desk to the right. He stood as we entered, nodded and whispered,

"Please tell me this means what I think it means, miss Virginia?"

"We can only hope, Sergeant," I said with a shrug.

To the left of the duty sergeant's desk, CJ stood in the open doorway of the Captain's office, impatiently waiting for an answer. When I peeked in over his shoulder, there sat Captain Charles James O'Leary, chief officer of the North Adams Constabulary, and not coincidentally my father. Fingers interlaced behind his head and leaning back, his chair springs groaned from the strain.

"Well, there ya' are. Doc and I were gettin' worried you two weren't goin' t' show. And you too Father."

The office filled with laughter as a short, rotund, but impeccably dressed figure spun half-way around in the visitor's chair in front of Da's desk to also greet us. But, once Doctor Samuel N. Briggs M. D. began, words seemed hardly able to flow from his mouth fast enough to keep up with his brilliant, agile mind.

"Just knew you two wouldn't be able to keep your noses out of this! Told the Captain here, 'Evidence reads clear as a book, Cap. Guaranteed CJ and Ginger will notice. And when they do ...'"

Certainly not wasting words to complete a thought whose answer he deemed obvious, Doc paused only long enough to take a breath and bore his eyes into both of us,

"Lawyers.... in an office... really! What were you two thinking? Getting those bastard mill owners off the hook when they finally get caught with dirt on their hands ... Knew it couldn't last ... just knew it!"

Doc then shook his head back and forth in mock disgust and tsk, tsked as he continued,

"By the by, nice to see you as well, Father Lynch. Glad you came along."

At that, Doc stood up and turned to face us straight on as he pulled a cheroot from his inside suit jacket pocket. He bit off the end and spat it out, adding punctuation and finality to his oration. However, the smug grin on his face evaporated, along with his aura of superiority, once he lit that awful thing and inhaled.

Da, CJ, Father Lynch and I all nearly blew the ceiling off the office as the comic relief provided by Doc coughing and hacking left him needing to grab his chair to regain stability.

Finally, somewhat recovered, Doc winked at CJ with still weepy eyes and said to me,

"What say you put on some coffee, missy, while the *men* talk business."

The office immediately went so quiet crickets living in the basement's musty corners could be heard chirping. I stepped around CJ, took two steps over and because I towered over him so, bent at the waist to meet Doc face to face and growled,

"You're lucky I love you, you nasty old man!"

As I turned to go find the stove, Doc called out,

"Will you think better of me if I get the next round?"

Father Lynch, who had quietly decided to give me a hand, laughed and said,

"I may grant you absolution, Doctor Briggs, but I doubt Virginia will!"

As the good father and I returned with five mugs of coffee, I found myself balking before crossing the office doorway threshold. Was it a sense of déjà vu... or was it nostalgia?

Da rocking back and forth in his chair behind his desk gazing out the basement window; Doc overflowing one of the two visitor's chairs, facing the captain's desk, chomping on his now extinguished cigar; and CJ standing with his back propped against the outside office wall, arms folded across his chest, searching for answers in the office floor. There was no question I *had* been here before. But there also was no question it *was* my favorite place to be.

And then it hit me...

Doc was right. I'm no lawyer, and never will be. And I'm certainly no dalaigh, no judge. An arbiter of truth requires the ability and willingness to weigh both sides of a dispute and determine what is best for the individuals involved, as well as society. It requires patience. It requires wisdom. And in America it requires the mastery of case law.

I've given my best to emulate you ... to be you, Seanmháthair Saorla. But my destiny cannot be yours. I need to confront the evil that lurks in men's souls. I need to force evil to look in the mirror.

I'm a detective.

Yes, you are and I'm proud of you...

"Ginger my dearest daughter, are you with us?"

Startled back from my musings by Da's voice, I sheepishly peeked around the room to find three smiling pairs of eyes patiently focused on me. But then there was also a fourth, belonging to Doc perched anxiously on the edge of his chair. Turned completely to face me and leaning heavily on the arm rest, Doc's trailing left leg nervously bounced up and down as he exclaimed,

"Well, want to know what the Captain and I have found out, or going to daydream all day? Gotta' get on with it, you know..."

I tried my best to return smiles to all around and quickly slipped into the open chair next to him, but Doc neither finished his sentence nor waited for my response. Instead he rose and said,

"What are you sitting down for, Virginia? Gotta' see the body, you know. That's where the answers are. What good's talking?"

Attempting to comply, I rose still holding my coffee cup. Doc shot me an exasperated glare and bellowed,

"What are you doing with that cup of mud? Won't be in your stomach long after you see what I have to show you."

Now it was my turn to roll my eyes!

"But, Doc, you're the one who ..."

"Never mind, miss Virginia, got answers to share ... You coming?"

Chapter 7
Empathy of a Different Kind

You bet! And so was everyone else. A left out of the office led down a short, dark corridor which emptied into a large room occupying the entire north-third of Constable Station's basement. Against the outer wall ran four thickly barred jail cells. Their small, above grade, and similarly barred windows admitted the sun's waning afternoon rays providing a somber, foreboding mood.

As my eyes nervously searched from one cell to the other, I noticed all the doors were open and the cells unoccupied, save one. To our left, the cell farthest from prying eyes was closed.

As we approached, Da struck matches and lit the gaslight wall sconces providing additional illumination. That made things a bit better. But that was also when I saw the bunk ... the white sheet covering it ... It must be the...

"Here we are, then, folks."

Without hesitation, Doc flung open the door which banged off the bars.

Don't any of the men in my life know how to open a door without breaking it?

Without either noticing, or maybe caring how small the cell was, Doc excitedly said,

"Step right in, folks!"

Da simply smiled, stepped aside, and with a sweep of his arm offered to usher the rest of us in. I looked nervously at CJ who returned only a nod and said,

"I think we can see just fine from out here, Doc."

Father Lynch, on the other hand, brushed by us, went directly to the shell that used to be Shayleigh Grogan, and genuflected by her side. Forthrightly, he reached under the sheet and fumbled about until he grasped her hand, exposing it for all to see.

"Forgive me, Shayleigh. Forgive me for thinking ... no, forgive me for *believing* you could take your own life."

Then he rose and made the sign of the cross over her shrouded body,

"Bask in the light of our Lord and the love of his Holy Mother this day and forever."

I'd forgotten the seriousness of the decision the good father had made in the eyes of many clerics to have performed the Sacrament of the Dead and given absolution to a soul destined to spend eternity in Hell. The good father's internal struggle must have been a crucial test of faith. His heart told him Shayleigh Grogan possessed a soul filled with goodness and love. But at the same time, his mind understood how she could have lost her faith. So, while it was true that suicide was the ultimate affront to God punishable by eternal damnation, he had chosen to follow his heart and taken it upon himself to know her state of mind before the end. The conditional absolution he'd administered had vouched for her to God and begged, in her stead, for forgiveness.

Father Lynch's soul-bearing actions and oration were so moving to all of us, even Samuel N. Briggs M.D., man of science and student of human weaknesses stood slack jawed.

Then, a resurrected Father Lynch turned to face all of us, smiled, but growled,

"Well, Doctor, what've ya' got? There's a son of a bitch out there who needs t' meet his maker!"

Shaking his head and smiling deferentially, a somewhat recomposed Doc Briggs picked up the mantle and resumed,

"Certainly are one of a kind, Father Lynch. Almost ... and I do say *almost,* tempt me to cross into the vestibule of St Francis, this Sunday morning. Could prove interesting!"

Given the setting, it seemed almost an irreverence to find amusement in Doc's predictable inability to admit emotional affect. But we couldn't help it. Each of us blurted a quick titter or short snort ... even his riv'rence himself.

It was simply too hard *not* to envision the brand new massive, gothic cathedral that was St. Francis of Assisi Church crashing down in both retribution and shock the moment Samuel N. Briggs M.D., man of science and student of human weaknesses crossed its threshold.

The momentary reverie was immediately sucked from the cell, however, when Doc pulled the sheet down exposing Shayleigh Grogan's tortured and broken head. The first things I noticed were her eyes. Hazy with death, they weren't closed. In fact, one was half closed while the other, wide open ... a black empty disc where color should have been, stared at me. And I wasn't prepared.

In an instant, a physical sensation originating in my most private of places rose through my torso and drove my heart to pounding so loudly I could sense it in my ears. Sucked into the abyss, my mind screamed,

Oh, God, no... NO! I'm not going to make it... I'm dy...

A hint of pain, just a pin prick really, and I was spinning out of control ... spinning more and more. And then all went black ... It was over.

When I opened my eyes, the first thing I saw was the ceiling. White, but grimy. Planks not plaster.

I'm not home.

The narrow bed was hard, the mattress thin. No blanket. No pillow. When I turned, bars surrounded me.

I'm on a bunk in a jail cell.

Oh no! I'm Shayleigh Grogan... I'm dead!

Still terrified, gripped by the after-effects of those last moments of Shayleigh's life ... Was it me? I shot to sitting bolt upright, grabbed my head with both hands and opened my mouth to scream, when ...

"Ginger...Ginger!"

That voice ... CJ!

And there he was. The love of my life. Down on a single knee next to my bunk, he smiled at me. It brought me back. I remembered who I was. And where I was. And why I was there.

I weakly returned CJ's smile and said,

"How long?"

"Not long. We're all still here."

They'd all seen it before. I never planned it. I never asked for it. But somehow, I'd inherited the ability, some say a gift, to feel the dead. Hear the dead.

Experience death without dying.

This time, though, I should have predicted that Shayleigh's spirit would reach out to me. After all, I'd experienced the death of another before. In the bowels of the Bloody Pit. I screamed at the crushing pain. Felt the despair of knowing I wasn't going to survive yet surviving to be an instrument of justice.

However, in the end, it didn't matter. The result would have been the same. I'd still be on this bunk. And then I suddenly realized ...

I knew ... I knew what happened ... I knew how Shayleigh Grogan died!

Chapter 8
Within the Sorrow

"Look in her ear, Doc. Check her ear!"

The words hadn't yet completely escaped my mouth as I vaulted from my cot and shot by my startled husband into Shayleigh's cell. I pointed down and exclaimed,

"There, see it?"

It took only a moment for the foursome of Doc, Da, CJ and the good father to abandon their positions surrounding my cot and join me in Shayleigh Grogan's cell. They all bent at the waist to peer more closely, but only Doc knelt down on one knee to reposition the poor girl's head.

The hair above her left ear was clotted with dried blood, indicating severe injury to that part of her skull. However, little of it had dripped by her ear or down the side of her face. A sure sign that the trauma to her skull had occurred after her heart ceased to function.

What there was was a trickle of pinkish gray syrup that had seeped from inside her ear and run down the side of her neck. I had seen something similar before. Just last spring as General Charles A. Cousins lay bleeding and dying at our feet in the bowels of the Hoosac Tunnel, a pinkish-gray suspension that was his brain had oozed from *his* ears.

But this was also different. Shayleigh's skull was not crushed and what trickled from her ear was only a rivulet of the stuff. She was alive when *this* injury was inflicted.

"Well, I'll be," Doc whispered.

He reached down and opened the scissor-mouth of his black bag. Rummaging about a bit, he emerged with what appeared to be a narrow-bladed metal spatula and a magnifying lens. Doc then proceeded to employ the spatula to expand Shayleigh's ear opening and the lens to examine the interior.

"Um... yes, yes. There it is. Deep inside, but it's there! Looks like she was stung by a very large wasp. Come everyone, have a look see."

Da clearly spoke for the other three men because they heartily nodded at his response,

"Just tell us, Doc."

Doc looked up at me and grinned wryly,

"Well, Virginia, why don't you tell them what happened?"

I wished I could. I really did. But I just stood as though frozen, Doc's prompt causing tears to begin running down my cheeks. For just a fleeting moment during the vision, Shayleigh and I had been one. I could no more report the method of Shayleigh Grogan's murder than I could my own. Because in a way, it was.

However, my tears were not of sorrow. They were an expression of the haunted feeling I was experiencing. The time for fighting was past. Shayleigh Grogan's despondent end had come, and I had been there. The hopelessness Shayleigh's spirit conveyed to me must have been painted across my face, because everyone seemed heedful ... save Doc. In situations such as this he had a maddening tendency to become lost in the world of science and deduction. To the exclusion of all else, he'd focus on symptoms as merely clues to solving a problem. While this trait made him the best physician for miles around, it also caused this normally good-hearted man to appear cold and bankrupt of empathy.

I'm sure Doc honestly believed he'd afforded me an opportunity to score credit for discovery of a clue. A tiny piece of me was even flattered. But in the end, all he really did was drive me within myself ... to that place only Saorla and I understood. It was only when CJ wrapped his consoling arms around me that Doc stepped back and finally contemplated what was going on around him.

"Yes ... Well ... Curiouser and curiouser, as the bard used to say. First examination revealed that the deceased had been restrained from the rear."

Still down on one knee Doc used his metal spatula as a pointer,

"See this purple mark surrounding the mouth? And these little red dots in the same area? These are called petechiae. Inside of the upper lip was cut a bit too from being pressed harshly against the teeth. Must've been a strong hand that was held across it. Sure evidence she was smothered."

Clearly uneasy, Doc paused before slowly rising. Lost in thought for only a moment, the smirk disappeared as he looked me in the eye.

"Had me confused, though. Didn't kill her. Heart was still pumping when she ... when she was ..."

At that Doc looked imploringly around the cell block for someone, anyone to say what only he knew needed to be said. Samuel N. Briggs, M.D. who had seen it all and laughed about it. What could possibly have stymied him? Maybe I knew:

Yes, Doc. Shayleigh could have been me. She was someone's daughter. A girl. A person.

I didn't have long to further ponder that question because Doc suddenly blurted out,

"Raped, she was! A virgin she was! Violated, defiled, soiled and only then did the bastard ram a shiv into her brain through her ear and end it all."

As disturbing as my vision had been, there *was* something worse than death, and Shayleigh had spared me that part of it.

Doc's spatula pinged as he threw in onto the cell's concrete floor, and with great disgust, growled,

"I need a drink."

Then brightening a bit continued,

"Let's all have a drink."

"And then let's find this prick and hang him from his balls!"

No one disagreed.

We adjourned to Da's office to settle our nerves and maybe make a bit of sense of it all. However, the next hour accomplished little except to demonstrate how wild rumors could so quickly permeate a community: minimal evidence, the human mind, and an empty bottle or two of Jameson. The more we drank, the wilder the scenarios became.

What kind of monster smothers a girl long enough to incapacitate her, but not extinguish the terror of being raped? How could anyone then mercilessly ram a shiv through her skull and into her brain? How cold-blooded is it to carry Shayleigh's corpse over his shoulder all the way to the top of Witt's ledge and toss her over in a crude attempt to mask the crime?

The images we conjured of the brute who could treat another human being like such a piece of garbage were worthless. The names we bandied about, slanderous.

We were going nowhere but home ... and CJ and I to face Jeremiah.

Chapter 9
More Pressing Matters

I was the first to walk in through the back door of the law offices, so I was the first one "greeted" by Jeremiah. Hands in his trouser pockets, he glared at me like I was a disobedient child, and began,

"I know where you've been, the whole village knows what happened."

And then pausing to take a deep breath ... struggling for restraint he couldn't muster, Jeremiah exploded,

"What I want to know. What I need to know, is how you expect to ever pass the bar exam next May? I've put my neck on the chopping block by sponsoring you to the Massachusetts Bar Association. Every colleague I talk to concludes our business with a postscript preaching to me about the folly of my actions. Three different judges ... THREE ... have summoned me into their chambers and offered stern admonishments. Each asked how I could possibly expect to be taken seriously by them when I had an obviously frivolous attitude toward the law."

Rolling his head back on his shoulders and blinking, Jeremiah implored the spirits of the ceiling before abruptly turning on his heel and stalking down the corridor toward his office. As he did, he bellowed so loudly I thought the walls would crumble,

"And the advice they have for YOU..."

That did it. I'd heard enough.

I turned to CJ, who had wisely refrained from any attempt at intervention. Raising an eyebrow, he quietly leaned against the corridor wall, arms crossed. Seeing the fire in my eyes, he shrugged and smiled,

"Go get him, Morrigan, goddess of death!"

So, I did.

"Jeremiah Colgrove the third, that's as far as you go!"

I stomped into Jeremiah's office, but rather than scream I stopped short, curtsied and in my best Irish lilt almost sang,

"Have I ever failed t' bow in def'rence, m'lord?"

And then building up a head of steam of my own, I growled,

"Would you have me believe that you never expected strong resistance, ridicule even, when *you* invited *me* to join your firm? Do you think I believe for one second that you didn't work your insufferable charm on even the judges? That by the time you left you had not only convinced them what you'd done wasn't only a good idea, but that each of them should search for their own female candidates to study for the bar?"

Then folding my hands in prayer, I bowed my head and continued,

"Grant me absolution, saint Jeremiah, for not being sensitive to your feelings ... for not giving a *shite* about your precious social position. But this isn't about *you*, you bloody gobshite! A young woman is dead, Jeremiah. Raped, murdered and tossed away like so much trash."

"So, for right now ... for the foreseeable future actually, that bloody exam is the furthest thing from my mind. Truth be told, I'm not sure I'll ever care as much as you do about me becoming a member of the Massachusetts Bar. In fact, I'm not sure I'll ever again care even a little bit."

Then, leaning forward and jutting my chin so that I was nose to nose with Jeremiah, I hissed,

"Solving Shayleigh Grogan's murder and bringing the animal who did this to expiation gives me life. It gives me purpose. And it's ..."

I found myself suddenly cut off when Jeremiah burst out,

"What's this? Raped? Murdered? The story circulating the village is the young girl cast herself off of Witt's Ledge!"

More than a little angered at Jeremiah's rudeness, it wasn't until I beheld his genuine look of dismay that I softened, took a deep breath, and calmly recounted the events of the day. In doing so I found myself, yet again, reliving the viciousness of the crime that had snuffed out Shayleigh Grogan's life. And I was exhausted.

At that, my whole being slumped. CJ reached out, placed a consoling hand on my back, and picked up the mantle,

"You see, Jeremiah? We can't walk away from this. The young woman didn't own much more than the clothes on her back. And, as far as we can tell, her lot in life had been cast to never do any better. Some would say she didn't have much of a life. But it was hers! In the end that's all any of us has."

Pausing, CJ closed his eyes and pursed his lips as he shook his head back and forth in solemn sadness,

"Who cries for Shayleigh Grogan? Who cares if we don't, Jer?"

"What kind of scum preys on the likes of Shayleigh Grogan?"

Seemingly moved by CJ's oration, Jeremiah deflated as he leaned back in his desk chair. However, his eyes belied his posture as they darted back and forth between us, his expression incongruously scornful.

"Well, counselor, you've certainly presented a persuasive case."

"But answer me this: Suppose you two pursue your quest and indeed swing this ... this evil doer. What then? Are you actually determined to waste your talents by wearing a navy-blue constable's uniform the rest of your life?"

"Counselor, you have the intelligence and ability to be a first-class solicitor. And you have something I don't have ... integrity. Folks trust you."

"I'm the best negotiator around. I can sell chicken manure to a chicken farmer. But in the end when I look a man in the eye and shake his hand, I somehow come across as perfidious. Sure, they'll make the deal with me, but they always come away checking their pockets to see if they've been robbed."

"What I'm saying, Conal, is I need you. I'm willing to give you and Ginger a ... um ... let's call it a furlough. Solve your little crime. But come back to work. Both of you."

Little crime? Grrrr...

"Jeremiah Colgrove. Listen to you! Did anything we've said actually penetrate that patrician skull of yours?"

"Listen, Ginger, I feel for the plight of the Shayleigh Grogans of this world. I really do. But there are hundreds just like her in the village, and more arriving every day. They live according to their station and there's really nothing I can do that will improve their lot."

"Face it, Ginger. She was probably out for a good time with one of her own, things got further along than she'd like, and the bloke killed her for refusing him."

"You bastard! One of her own? And that would be ... what? A human being?"

Was that CJ who just said that?

He'd tried only once before to come between Jeremiah and me in an argument and was promptly dispatched by both of us. But not this time. And use a curse word? In CJ's mind Jeremiah must have *really* crossed the line. The business world was darkening Jeremiah's kind heart. I didn't know this man, and obviously neither did CJ!

For more than a few moments nothing was said. We'd all said quite enough. Finally, CJ and I turned on our heels, went back up the corridor, climbed the stairs to our apartment on the second floor, and left Jeremiah alone and brooding behind his upper-class desk.

Chapter 10
Solution to the Problem (Maybe)

The next morning CJ and I were dressed and out the door before Jeremiah arrived. I don't think he wanted another confrontation with us any more than we did with him. After all, Jeremiah had every right to be furious with us. For quite a while now he'd been suppressing his temper with me for dodging my studies, and with CJ for enabling my behavior. We had let him down.

A law firm, after all, was a business, and Jeremiah a business lawyer. His accounts included not only his father's extensive holdings, but also those of several of the most influential textile mill owners in western Massachusetts. And in one fell swoop the law firm of *Colgrove and Mulcahy* had been diminished by two-thirds.

However, it was more than leaving Jeremiah overwhelmed by the volume of work to be done. We could be replaced in a heartbeat. There were lawyers throughout Berkshire County who would pay Jeremiah for the opportunity to work for him. His contacts alone meant stature and wealth, lots of wealth!

It was the dashing of a dream. Jeremiah and I had been inseparable friends since childhood. And from the first day they met last year, Jeremiah and CJ had become inseparable friends who forged a bond based upon their complimentary attributes.

Jeremiah Colgrove III is over six feet tall and could have modeled for Michelangelo's statue of David. This, together with his dark hair, piercing eyes and impeccable dress, carved a figure impressive to women and intimidating to men. In business dealings, Jeremiah certainly was his father's son: cold, calculating and feared as much as respected. However, he faints at the sight of blood, and when feeling threatened employs people to ensure his personal safety.

CJ is five feet eight and borders on emaciated. He's a rumpled dreamer who, in spite of having his left leg shredded by Confederate shrapnel and would at the time have killed without compunction the man who fired the shot; would also embrace him if they met today.

For Conal John Mulcahy, morality and ethics are guiding principles of life. His sense of duty and justice make him, to me, larger than life. For Jeremiah they're situational. Legality is the guiding principle of *his* life and, as far as Jeremiah is concerned, even that could be bent a bit if need be. Together they forged a powerful and successful legal team. But today that team is no more.

Because of its proximity, we decided to walk to the constable station. Not being on horseback, I had the luxury of safely looking around as we emerged from the alley between the Colgrove block and the Adams Savings Bank building on our left. While I thoroughly admired the opulent beauty of the Savings Bank building and its marble interior, I was instantly struck by the irony of where I stood. As soon as I turned east and beheld the majestic spires of the Congregational, Baptist and Methodist churches atop Church Hill, I couldn't help but pause for a second and chuckle.

Colgrove and Mulcahy, Counselors at Law, and solicitors to the powerful, occupied the well-heeled building strategically placed directly between the palace captains of industry had built to hoard the wealth they'd accrued during the week, and the edifices where they prayed to God for forgiveness on Sundays because of how they'd gotten it.

As I turned back from gazing up at Church Hill I beheld the ever patient CJ waiting for me. My introspective musings were always discernible to him by the extended moments of silence, accompanied by a distant stare that often came over me. He knew better than to ask what was on my mind. Experience had taught him he probably didn't want to know. So, he changed the subject before the subject had been established.

"How long will it take for Jeremiah to forgive us, Virginia?"

Shaken from my thoughts and obviously confused, he went on,

"I've seen *you* have a dust-up with him, but *I've* never been part of one. And to be honest, I'm worried. He's a grand friend, almost a brother. I guess I should be asking you *if* he'll get over it."

I pondered that for a moment and then answered,

"Jeremiah first and foremost is a pragmatist. From the very earliest days, our friendship sprang from the reality that no one else wanted anything to do with us."

I laughed as I continued,

"And on more than one occasion we couldn't even stand each other. We went days without talking. However, there also was, and still is, a deep affection for one another which has always compelled reconciliation. Of this I *am* sure, Conal; Jeremiah cares as much for you as he does for me. So, he'll come around. Just give it time ... and for heaven's sake, don't dwell on it!"

At that, Conal nodded, wanly smiled, and took my hand. As we began our walk, I couldn't help reflecting upon how glorious New England mornings in October could be. Cold crisp westerly breezes greeted us while the morning sun still rising into the cloudless sky warmed our backs. At the same time, it saddened me that the purpose of this walk was to begin the task of bringing to justice the evil soul responsible for robbing a young, penniless Irish immigrant girl of one of the few things in life she was free to enjoy ... drinking in the wonderful, pure air of an early October morning.

It was only one block to the corner of Bank Street before we turned south. There, on the crown of the knoll not far away, stood the starkly plain, brick mausoleum that was our destination, Village Hall; and to the rear, in its basement, Constable Station.

When CJ opened the door, we were greeted by a beaming Sergeant Smart who rose from his desk to greet us.

"We got the sons o' bitches, CJ!"

Incredulous and speechless, I almost throttled CJ's left arm. As he glanced over his shoulder at me, the look I beheld on his face understated his response,

"Elisha, what the ... what are ya' talking about, man? Got who? How? When?"

Sergeant Smart raised his hand in front of him showing us his palm. At first, I thought he was trying to halt CJ's staccato list of questions so he could begin to answer them. But the deep breath he took in and let out as he plopped back down in his desk chair clearly demonstrated that he really wished he could go back in time and rephrase his greeting to us.

"The Captain has the Ingersoll brothers in his office. Got hauled in last night for trying to roll a drunk coming out of the North Adams House saloon. Wasn't their first of the evening either. The beat constables were paired up and already on the prowl for these two blokes because they knocked around old Harley Meeker earlier in the evening and took his bottle from him."

"Anyhow, as Constable Thayer and his partner passed an alleyway not far from the saloon, they heard moaning. When they investigated, they found the Ingersolls busted up pretty good and bleeding. The interesting thing, though, is the older brother, Terence, wasn't just busted up;

he was also gut-stuck by an awl that the constables found on the ground at the scene."

"Sergeant Hawes was the one who filled me in on all this when I came on duty this morning. He also told me that when he went looking for Doctor Briggs, he found him over at the Wilson House saloon where he was holding court as usual. When Hawes saw the number of empty glasses on the table, he figured he was going to have a tough time of it. But the good doctor was quite gracious... and surprisingly lucid. Came right over and patched both of the gobs up. They're sore and Terence's wound is still leakin' a bit, but they'll live."

"This brings me back to my blathered greeting, CJ. The Ingersolls named Freddie Pym as the man they tried to roll. They figured the two of them could handle him."

As the outside door behind us banged off the wall startling both CJ and me, Sergeant Smart rose again from his chair and looking beyond us toward the doorway chortled,

"Obviously they were wrong. Freddie Pym? They must've already finished off old Harley's bottle to try that one. Freddie's as big as the mountain he lives on and just as wild."

Before we were able to turn, Doc Briggs was standing between us and reaching up, placed one hand on each of our nearer shoulders and roared,

"So, Elisha, how're my patients doin? Still vertical?"

Chomping his stogie and looking back and forth at CJ and me, Doc didn't wait for an answer he already knew, and instead asked,

"So, you two ready to join the fun?"

Doc was already on his way to the door to Da's office when CJ ran the three steps to our left, intercepting him. He grabbed the knob and with his back against the door faced Doc with a mock terrified look on his face. Raising his index finger to his lips, he whispered,

"Shhhh! Why don't you let me open 'er up, Doc?"

Sergeant Smart and I both struggled to suppress laughing because we knew what the chain of events allowing Doc Briggs open that door would trigger. Doc raised both of his hands in surrender and grinned as he chomp, chomped his unlit cigar from one side of his mouth to the other.

CJ gently knocked and then warily poked his head through the opened door.

"About time, CJ," Da called out. "I suppose the other two are right behind ya'. Well, come on in. Wait 'll ya' hear what these two gobshites have been tellin' me."

When we entered the office, Da beamed as he rocked back in his chair and clasped his hands behind his head. The Ingersolls occupied the visitor's chairs Doc and I usually used, so we ambled around to get a better view. Doc leaned against Da's desk while I joined CJ against the outer wall of the office. Once we were situated, Da continued,

"Let me introduce ya' to Terence and Jasper Ingersoll, two of the stupidest fools in all o' North Adams. Terence is the one leakin' his guts all over m' floor. Jasper's the one who used t' have a nose and is lookin' at us through those purple slits where his eyes used t' be."

I was tempted to laugh at what Da had said, but the sight of both of these gobs made me queasy instead. Terence and Jasper looked like they were survivors of a train wreck. Their clothes were torn and covered with mud. Jasper's bandaged right arm was in a sling. His exposed fingers were swollen like sausages and as purple as his eyes. He chewed on his bottom lip every few seconds and winced with pain. While it was obvious that Terence's face had also been pummeled by some incredible force, it was instead pale and drained. Clearly it was a struggle for him to even remain conscious.

Doc must have caught the shocked look on my face because he chortled as he almost gleefully punctuated the scene with,

"You should have seen them last night."

CJ, neither smiling nor shocked, dispassionately continued,

"Their condition is evidence of their stupidity, Cap. Why should we believe a word they say? We're supposed to believe that Freddie Pym did this much damage ... by himself? Freddie may be a hulk, but he's one of the most inoffensive visitors to the village we have. Comes down off the mountain once a month driving a buckboard laden with wares he and his family built and sells them to the Adams brothers at their cabinet shop. Spends the night quietly getting blind drunk ... maybe gets his knob polished too, although there's never been any talk of that. But he always begins his trek back up the mountain shortly after daybreak the next morning. He's usually gone before anyone knows he's been here."

Da rose up from his chair and approached Jasper Ingersoll. He bent over at the waist until he was eyeball to eye slit with him and said,

"Ah, CJ, so good to have ya' back. Nothing makes a copper better at his job than t' have a lawyer put a new angle on his reasoning. What say, Jasper?"

Da straightened up, cuffed Jasper Ingersoll lightly behind his left ear and demanded,

"Well?"

Da didn't wait more than a second or two before continuing. I don't really think he expected or wanted an answer this soon. He was having too much fun.

"Sergeant Mulcahy here says you're a lyin' sack o' shite, Ingersoll. And he's got me thinkin' he may be right. Why *should* we believe you or your brother?"

Then Da stepped behind Terence who visibly cringed as Da began massaging his shoulders,

"Maybe it was you two who raped Shayleigh Grogan and tossed her body off Witt's ledge. But then again, maybe it was *you* who got rolled. Lord knows, after swilling down that bottle o' lightning you stole from ol' Harley Meeker, you must've been pretty lit. And when you pulled that shiv you were carryin', Terry, it got turned back on ya'."

Da cuffed on the back of Ingersoll's head as he walked back to his desk, sat down, and leaning forward glared at the brothers:

"Maybe you're both lying t' save your sorry arses from the rope. Well? What've ya' got t' say? Convince the good counselor here ... Why the fook should any of us believe ya'?"

At that the Ingersoll brothers locked glances and would have fled their chairs if either one was physically able. It was Terence who first spoke,

"Whoa there, gen'ral, what are you talking about here? I thought we was here because we ruffed up Harley Meeker t'get his hooch. No one didn't say nothin' about no murder!"

Then Jasper croaked,

"Who's Shayleigh Grogan?"

Infuriated by the Ingersolls' response, Da shot from his chair. He was right before Jasper, drawing back his fist, when he was deflected by an equally quick CJ who seized his arm before he could finish the job of closing Jasper's eyes.

"Don't bother hurting your hand on these chancers, Captain."

Da glared at CJ but said nothing. He plodded over to his office door and threw it open. The glass rattled as the door rebounded off the wall. Then he bellowed,

"Sergeant Smart. Get these two ... these two ... sleeveens out a' my sight. Lock 'em up!"

After Elisha led the Ingersoll brothers down the corridor to the cell block, Captain O'Leary immediately softened, gave his door the once over, checking for damage, and softly closed it. When he turned back, Da was smiling broadly. CJ and Doc Briggs burst into raucous laughter. Only after I thought these two would bust a gut did Doc manage to say,

"Nice to see you haven't lost your touch, Cap. And as for you, CJ, you can't tell me this isn't more fun than business law."

CJ visibly flushed as Da walked over and draping his arm around my love's shoulders continued,

"Glad you arrived on time there, m' boy. I might've hurt m' hand on Jasper's empty skull if ya' hadn't."

I just stood there, arms crossed, shaking my head. After all, I'd seen it all before.

Men and their childish games. Sometimes I wonder if any of them ever grow up!

It was only after a few more moments of revelry that Da joined Doc leaning against his desk. He reached back bracing himself against the desktop as he asked,

"Well what do ya' think? What's the truth of it? Did the Ingersolls get rolled? Are they coverin' their arses by blaming poor Freddie Pym? Or did Freddie really pound the ever livin' shite out'a those two?"

It was Doc who then chimed in,

"And who owns that bloody shiv? That's the key."

Da pointed right at Doc and continued,

"Exactly. That's our murderer, folks."

It was CJ who stated the obvious:

"There's only one way to find out. We've got to bring Freddie in for a chinwag."

At that the office fell completely silent. Uneasy glances were exchanged back and forth... then all around.

All I got was confused. And my quizzical look must have showed because Doc cryptically offered,

"I take it, Ginger, you've never been to Notchboro."

Chapter 11
Notchboro

I may never have been to Notchboro before, but if our preparations to go there were any indication ...

Sergeant Smart was sent to fetch Father Lynch, CJ and I to saddle Killian and Hessie. Upon our return, we saw that in our absence Da had procured a pair of double-barreled shotguns and a box of ammunition from the weapons' vault. As we waited for his riv'rence to arrive with Elisha, Da checked the operation of each unloaded weapon. Sighting at some invisible enemy, he pulled the triggers and called out, "Bam, bam!" each time the falling hammers gave their reassuring clicks.

I was more than a bit taken aback by the sight of Da absently smiling at each weapon as he lovingly polished it with a cloth before setting it down on his desk. Da never went hunting! In fact, the only gun at the farm was kept in the barn and Stanley was the only one I'd ever seen use it, either to kill a varmint or to put down an animal in pain. It had never occurred to me that *Da* knew how to use a gun.

And it made me shiver to imagine that he may have needed to in the past.

Uncharacteristically silent, Doc paced about the office chomping feverishly on his cigar. His trepidation obvious, Doc's eyes flitted back and forth from Da, to the guns, to CJ, to me.

Wasn't it only a short while ago that Doc kidded me about going t' Notchboro?

Da, on the other hand, appeared relaxed. Leaning against his desk, he was clearly enjoying the prospects of visiting Notchboro. When a knock on the door finally broke the tension, the Captain stole a quick glance at CJ and me, winked, and called out,

"Enter."

And enter he did. Father Charles Lynch in full regalia. Smiling broadly at all of us, he took a full turn and chuckled,

"Well, what do ya' think?"

Flowing black cassock, Roman collar so high and so starched the good father's head appeared propped on it, rather than attached to the torso wearing it. A gold Celtic cross dangled freely from the chain hanging about his neck.

Before any of us could remark, the good father smirked, raised one admonishing index finger in front of him and the hem of his cassock with the other. Revealed from beneath the formal trappings of Reverend Charles E. Lynch, pastor of St. Francis of Assisi Parish, North Adams, Massachusetts was the real Charles Lynch, late of Ballyjamesduff, Ireland, wearing the ankle high work boots and coarsely woven breeches of a farmer.

Everyone burst out laughing, even Doc.

Am I the only one who hasn't a clue?

Evidently, there was a lot I didn't know. Of course, Da, CJ and I mounted our horses skillfully. And after what I'd learned in the past twenty-four hours about the good father, I wasn't surprised at all when he unceremoniously hoisted up his cassock and nimbly climbed on. But, when I turned around and found Doc already sitting proudly upon his mount, casually patting his horse's shoulder, I almost fell off mine!

Doc must have anticipated my start because he almost too casually removed his cigar from his mouth, flicked it to the ground and grinning at me said,

"Can't take the chance of swallowing any of that blasted tobacco juice while bouncing around on this old plug, now can I?"

I could only shake my head and return his smile as I turned back.

Since everyone in our group but me had been to Notchboro before, I had no choice but to hang back and follow. Da may have given me a general idea where we were headed, but it was the condition of the Ingersolls and the shotguns he and CJ carried across their laps that more than hinted what it was like there. So, I was more than happy to bring up the rear ... and Doc's position only a bit ahead told me he agreed.

The first leg of our route took us directly back to Witt's Ledge. As we gazed up at the cold, naked stone of the quarry's face, each of us became lost in our own rendering of yesterday's events. So, this time Freddie Pym was a player in my mind's eye. Sure, and I'd encountered him about the village before. But I'd never felt threatened. Never sensed evil of any sort, let alone the depravity required to murder Shayleigh Grogan and then toss her from the cliff two hundred feet above me.

Still, it *had* happened. Freddie Pym *was* a powerful man and even though I hadn't sensed evil, anger or guile in his aura, still waters often run deep. And truth be told, I was unsure of my abilities to bring his true nature to the surface.

Before we passed, Father Lynch held up his hand and called out to all of us,

"D'ya' think we might pause here for a moment? I'd like t' offer a prayer."

Without waiting for our answer, and without preamble, Father Lynch crossed himself and began,

"On Terra in this fateful hour
I place all Heaven with its power
the sun with its brightness
the snow with its whiteness
the fire with all the strength it hath
the lightning with its rapid wrath
the winds with their swiftness along their path
the sea with its deepness
the rocks with their steepness
the earth with its starkness
all these I place
With God's almighty help and grace
between myself and the powers of darkness."

Father then crossed himself again and bowed his head. It was the only way we could know he'd finished. I, for one, had never heard a prayer like it. The quizzical looks we shared with each other told me Da, CJ and Doc hadn't either. We each offered a stumbling,

"Amen," and prepared to resume our trek.

As we got under way, curiosity got the better of me. I nudged Hessie ahead so I could ride next to Father Lynch. After a minute or so I summoned the courage to inquire about the blessing he'd offered.

"Your riv'rence, I've never heard a blessing quite like this one."

We continued for a while in silence as Father Lynch considered his response:

"Of this I am sure, Virginia Daelyr; Shayleigh Grogan is now with Jesus, Mary and all the saints. She requires no further assistance from us. On the other hand, our struggle against the forces of darkness and evil continues. Right now, our journey may be takin' us t' confront its incarnation. St. Patrick simply reminds us that we can never have enough help in that endeavor. So, I thought this nearly pagan prayer he gave us was an appropriate choice."

Now I was even more confused. St. Patrick was the Catholic patron saint of Ireland. What could he embrace of its ancient pagan past? But before I could inquire further, Fr. Lynch expanded his thoughts:

"Ya' see, Ginger, at the time St. Patrick arrived, the Irish had worshipped many pagan gods for over a thousand years. So, when Christian missionaries showed up on the Irish shores, the teachings of Jesus were seen as just one more god t' be venerated. Christianity may have stood on an equal footing with Druidism in most of Ireland, but that was as far as it went."

"Patrick himself was born inta' this culture. And while he later came to embrace Roman Catholicism and dedicate the rest of his life t' spreadin' it throughout Ireland, he never forgot the beauty of his pagan roots. In fact, this is one o' the reasons King Laoghaire trusted Patrick t' work with him when he saw the wisdom in reconcilin' Irish law with the laws o' the Catholic Church."

The good father then chuckled a bit and said,

"And a good job of it they did too, Virginia, because the Senchus Mor has survived in Ireland to this day."

We hadn't gone much farther before the road we were on took an abrupt turn up the side of the foothills of Ragged Mountain and became little more than a path. Forced to ride single file and leaning forward to accommodate for the slope, all conversations came to an end. Eventually the road leveled off. It also began bending gently to the right following the contour of the land.

It was then I noticed that the bustling village of North Adams had vanished behind us. The ambient din created by hundreds of voices going about their daily business. The teams of horses pulling wagons laden with goods jingling from one store to another. The growling locomotives which labored to drag their trains clack, clacking over steel rails through the village. The acrid odor and taste of sulfurous, dusty air created by village activities which both insulted our lungs and permeated our clothes. All gone. All had been replaced by the rustling of leaves moved by mountain breezes, the chirping songs of birds, and the almost mesmerizing lullaby of running water. Beautiful.

It was as if we were being swallowed up by a pastoral other-world. The world the first settlers saw. Ragged mountain rose precipitously to our left while Mount Williams loomed higher, yet more gently to our right. The notch formed at the point of their joining to the south must have been the source of the running-water song I'd been listening to. Before me, cascading down over the rocks and boulders was neither a tiny burbling stream nor a roaring river. It was as unique as this place. In the hollow at its base was a large pond. At first, I thought it had been formed by a beaver dam. But as we got closer, I could see a very large, gently turning water wheel embedded in a rock and boulder dam. Invisible until we were nearly on top of it, it was the first sign of life we'd encountered in over two miles. This must be Notchboro.

    I was quite relaxed and enjoying the stunning beauty of my surroundings when I sensed, more than heard, the sudden ripping of leaves above our heads. A nearly simultaneous ba-boom in the distance followed which echoed off the mountains. Our startled horses immediately reacted according to their personalities. Rusty and Killian reared on their back legs as Da and CJ struggled to rein them in. Hessie, turned to flee back down the mountain, but ran right into Doc's rented horse which was so old it barely reacted at all. By the time we'd regained control and calmed our horses down, Father Lynch had already steadied his mount and was riding forward. Holding his pectoral cross high above his head and standing in his stirrups he called out loudly,

    "Jubal Pym, is that you? Jubal? Come now, man, put that musket away! I've come t' minister to the clan, and these folks with me have come to have a talk with ya'."

There was a protracted silence punctuated only by the sound of the good father's horse as it clomped on. He hadn't gotten far before a powerful voice ordered,

"Ya'all hold it right thar', Rev'rend. I'm comin' out."

Evidently satisfied, Father Lynch pulled up on his horse, sat back down in his saddle and prepared to wait. I squinted into the distance in an attempt to focus on where I believed Jubal Pym to be but saw only a curtain of trees. Then I heard a click to my left and barely a second later another on my right. Suddenly more than a bit on edge, I snapped around to locate the sources of the sounds. At first all I could see was tall, wispy hay grass running along the side of the road which merged with the dense forest behind it. It was only when voices attached themselves to the clicks that I finally was able to detect the very long, very thin barrels of two muzzle loading long rifles pointing at us from behind the trees.

First from our left, "You'd best drop 'em on the ground right now."

And then from our right, "Or we'll drop you."

The tone of the voices was quite cold and threatening, almost inviting us to test them. Seemingly unperturbed at being outflanked, Da slid the gun off his lap and grinned at CJ who returned the smile and winked at me as he dropped his. Neither armed nor relaxed, Doc slowly raised his hands above his head.

The voice to our left guffawed loudly and then sighed,

"Put yur hands down, Doc. You'd be the last one we'd expect to have a gun."

And then from our right,

"Cap'n, you an' Sarge there got any more guns on ya'?

When Conal and Da both shook their heads, the voices emerged from the forest and nodded. They both stood smiling at us, their muskets at the ready but pointed only at the sky.

Now I was *completely* confused. These men who'd only a few minutes ago had me convinced they'd like nothing better than to shoot us, now seemed more a welcoming committee than sentinels ... for maybe a minute or so. As soon as I became comfortable with that notion, a very dour man, casually carrying a very large rifle in the crook of his right arm emerged from the forest cover some twenty or so yards in front of us.

"Reverend, you and the Cap'n know the way. Let's get on with it."

And so, we did. Very slowly. As we reached the dam a gentle mist filled the air as water splashed over the wheel's paddles and cascaded into a rock lined channel leading to a stream. The water wheel groaned and creaked as its axle ground against the dam's stone cradle. A long extension of the axle penetrated the wall of a large building situated next to the dam. The vertical wood siding was so greyed and weathered it blended into the landscape. Add to that a steeply pitched roof shingled in coarsely split shakes nearly covered by moss mats, and the building virtually became part of the forest.

No wonder I hadn't seen it. The high-pitched whine from within the building and the sweet aroma in the air of freshly sawn wood gave up its purpose. I'd already known the Pyms were furniture makers, and this was their sawmill. The labor-intensive transformation of logs harvested from the surrounding mountains into the fine furniture they produced began here.

Once by the sawmill, the path turned south toward the notch and led up a gentle slope. It was only a matter of yards before Jubal Pym turned, and showing us his left palm ordered us to halt. After Father Lynch dismounted, the rest of us took our cue and followed suit. Our horses were immediately taken in charge by our sentries and led away to a pasture to graze.

  My attention was drawn to the beauty of the dammed pond which was now below us and to our left. Mountain fall foliage reflected off the water's surface and shimmered as breezes riffled the surface. It was edged by a wide swath of gently sloping land open to the sky. Only when I focused did I notice that the pattern of vegetation lacked the random character of nature. Row after row of cultivated turnips, carrots, potatoes, and beans populated the space. Because these crops were interspersed with the native grasses, there was very little raw earth exposed. It seemed that in this area of abundant water and fertile soil the gardeners not only didn't weed their crops, they encouraged their growth. Maybe to prevent erosion? Maybe to give forest browsers something other than their crops to munch on? Before I could speculate further, my eye was drawn still farther south where a large grove of apple trees stood in the distance.

  The residents of Notchboro were not going to starve, even during the harshest of Berkshire winters. These crops were hardy and stored well, not to mention they tasted darned good too.

Midday became a false dusk as soon as Jubal led us to our right and under the forested canopy of the foothills of Mt. Williams. Only a kaleidoscope of light penetrated the orange, yellow and red treetops and the resultant drop in temperature caused me to shiver. Once my eyes adjusted, I beheld the heart of Notchboro.

There, a warren of paths climbed the gentle mountain slope and had at the terminus of each branch a pocket of removed understory vegetation with its own cabin and outhouse standing in the middle. Every single dwelling had managed to be situated atop a hillock so that there was at least a bit of level ground surrounding it. Beyond that, there was no pattern to their placement. The lodges were constructed of the same materials as the sawmill, had a stone fireplace on one sidewall and a small workshop attached to the other. Without a doubt, the residents of Notchboro had applied their woodworking skills to their abodes. While their homes may have lacked the conveniences we in the village took for granted, they were well constructed and snug.

But that's where the clan's idyllic façade evaporated.

No one was there. Not one home had an occupant. The hearths wisped hints of smoke, but workshop doors were ajar, creaking back and forth in the breeze. I suddenly recalled that as we passed the dam I may have heard the whine of the mill's massive blade, but no actual work was being done with it ... only the remnant aroma of travails shortly past wafted through the air. Not one person was in the garden tending the crops. No cows, sheep, chickens or goats.

In fact, there weren't any of the noises one would associate with village life.

And most eerily ... no voices. None at'all ...

Just then, Jubal broke my spell by reminding us *he*, at least, was still around ... and still in charge.

"Up there."

Back from tending our horses, our two guards had also seemed to re-materialize from the zephyr. Now flanking our group, they reinforced Jubal's command by making prodding motions with the barrels of their muskets.

Our only choice was a narrow path which seemed to lead nowhere but up the side of the mountain. Nonetheless, off we went. Father Lynch, Doc Briggs and Da went first. CJ dropped back to accompany me. Once side by side, he whispered in my ear,

"Well, *this* never happened before!"

My withers suddenly tingling, I turned my head in an attempt to discern any hints of concern projected on CJ's face. All I saw were sparkling eyes and a face grinning like the cat who'd just swallowed a canary.

Agggghhhhh, damn you, Conal John!

"Listen, Virginia, if they didn't want us here, we'd have been turned away long ago. Just relax and go with it. Trust me, the Pyms are good people."

CJ then stifled a chuckle as he added,

"But they do have their ways."

Following the contours of the hill, we meandered along for a good ten minutes before approaching the crown of a foothill. Spread out still a bit above us was a fairly large open pasture whose boundaries were clearly defined by a knee-high rubble-stone wall. I was in the process of wondering why the Pyms hadn't chosen here to settle when rows of nondescript wooden crosses filling the space became apparent, along with forty or so men, women and children who stood together glowering at us.

Chapter 12
Freddie Pym

A small, grizzled figure limped forward from the group and met us a few yards outside the graveyard entrance. My first impression was that life had worn on this man ... hard. His straw-like hair was long and tied back into a careless plait which draped along humpbacked shoulders. The tiny area of his face not covered by a full beard revealed pale, pasty colored skin. His eyes were drawn, conveying the pain he must be feeling with every movement. He leaned heavily upon a cane attempting to provide the support his bowed legs could not. The black suit he wore was rumpled and threadbare. Clearly, this man didn't have much time left on earth and the precious resources of the clan weren't to be wasted on him. It was equally clear he didn't care.

When he finally spoke, his voice was high-pitched, nearly a screech, and as graveled as his appearance.

"Freddie tol' us what happened, so we've been expectin' ya'. You mean's t' take 'im away an' we cain't let that happen. He's clan and that's all there's to it."

He then turned his back to us and staggered back among his people.

Before any of us could react to what just occurred, Jubal Pym assumed the place before us and continued,

"Why'nt you folks join us."

Once we reached the confines of the cemetery walls, Jubal held his gun in what a soldier would call the port arms position and said,

"Hold it right there."

He then seemed to sneak a peek over his shoulder before very quietly explaining,

"Elder Cyrus Pym's position t'day is largely a courtesy, a sign of respect. But when he was named head of the clan some seventy years ago, his word was final. The Pym clan of Notchboro policed, rewarded and punished its own."

Jubal paused long enough to again check over his shoulder that we were his only audience before resuming,

"But today he's failing badly. You'd do well to 'member that while words may be spoke by Elder Cyrus, actions 'll come from me."

Jubal was a new breed of elder; pragmatic enough to understand the growing interdependence between Notchboro and North Adams but struggling with his responsibility to clan history. My best guess was that while the clan perception might have been that the purpose of our presence was to confab about Freddie's role in the condition of the Ingersolls, Jubal was fully aware that the questions which needed answering involved another incident entirely ... an incident too serious to be left to clan justice, the murder of Shayleigh Grogan. And Jubal Pym was willing to bet his emerging prestige and position within the clan on the fairness of Captain O'Leary.

Jubal then turned to face his family, and holding his musket in one hand raised it high above his head and proclaimed,

"Freddie Pym ... These good folks 've come to talk with you. Come forth and be heard."

At that, all members of the clan quietly flowed to the outer-reaches of the cemetery, save one. Alone in the middle of the cemetery, cowering before us, was the man-child Freddie Pym.

Taken aback at first, I stole a quizzical glance at CJ who simply smiled and gave me that, "C'mon, think," look. When I turned back it struck me. Jubal Pym had just parted the waters of a solemn, almost prayerful can while standing on the shore of the final resting place of the clan's ancestors.

Notchboro's culture must be based upon a melding of Puritan Christianity with the veneration of their forbears! I'll bet every tenet of their society is based upon some folktale ... and I'll bet they come here to pray to their forefathers for guidance. I'll bet they bring their children here when it's time to pass this knowledge to the new generation. I'll bet ...

"Ow! What was that for?"

As I looked down at CJ, I already knew the answer. I must have been lost in my thoughts again, projecting that vacant, distant stare. Damn!

CJ tilted his head to the side and murmured more than spoke,

"I don't know where you were, Ginger, but I want you to take a good look at Freddie. What do we really know about him?"

"What do you mean, Conal?" I whispered back. "He's a fixture of the North Adams community, isn't he? Comes off the mountain and spends the weekend downstreet once a month."

"Sure, and he does," CJ answered. "Just like clockwork. Brings the wagonload of furniture the Pym family has made. Delivers it to the cabinet shop on North Church and Eagle. One of the Adams brothers pays him. Freddie then drives the wagon just down the street to Millard's general store. George takes payment and gives Freddie whatever's left over. With those few dollars Freddie spends the night. Usually gets drunk, finds a room and sleeps it off. Picks up the clan's stores at Millard's the next morning and quietly heads back up the mountain."

CJ took a second to look around before continuing,

"But the man has no friends. Keeps completely to himself. I never knew one person who ever had a conversation with him, not even Millard or the Adams brothers. They've all mentioned to me at one time or another that he's so quiet that they've turned around and were shocked to be face to face with him. He was just there. Really strange, don't you think?"

CJ's abridgment of Freddie Pym certainly gave me pause. The man seemed to be a flesh and blood ghost to me too, but not quite ... simply because I'd spent so little time downstreet before CJ and I had been married.

"What we *do* know ... at least what you've told me, Conal, is he's often badly teased ... but until now has never reacted. And it seems the only reason he did *this* time was because those two sleeveens Jasper and Terence cornered him. They really left him no choice."

"True, but keep in mind, Ginger, we're not here because he pounded the tar out of the Ingersolls. We need to determine if Freddie Pym's a cold, calculating murderer. God knows, he's strong enough ... and Witt's ledge is right on Freddie's way home. And the murder weapon *is* a common cabinet maker's tool. But does Freddie Pym have murder in his heart? Look at him."

It was then that the sun's mid-afternoon rays were cut off, covering my face in shadow. I immediately knew the source of this solar eclipse but turned anyhow to face an exasperated Captain O'Leary glaring at us.

"If you two don't mind, I'd like to ask a question or two of our suspect so we might find out of few things."

CJ and I winced at each other. Da shook his head in exasperation and called out across the cemetery,

"Freddie Pym, what can you tell me about your altercation last night with Jasper and Terence Ingersoll?"

Seconds passed without an answer from Freddie. He continued to stare at the ground, and obviously frightened, simply stood there quaking. In fact, he didn't seem to have heard the question. So, Da asked again,

"Freddie ...

When the only response came from the intensifying grumbles of clan members angered by one of their own being subjected to the inquisition of an intruder, Jubal stepped in,

"Freddie, you kin trust Captain O'Leary. Just tell 'im what happened."

Freddie looked up at Jubal, faced all of us, and with imploring eyes blurted out,

"B'deep d'dip dip ... woooeee! Woooeee ... woooeee!

Chapter 13
Simplicity of Innocence

My gosh! What was THAT?

"Ginger, you look like a freshly landed trout."

It was CJ.

I closed my gaping mouth and was reeling my eyes back into my head as I happened to notice Doc. He was veritably beaming as he pulled a cheroot from his vest pocket with one hand and popped a wooden match to life with the thumbnail of the other.

Jubal had already approached Freddie and was quietly comforting him. Beside me, Father Lynch mumbled what could only have been a prayer. As a group, the Pyms are the strong, capable, fetching people. Their village is idyllic, almost ethereal. Their furniture is beautifully finished. The growing worker population of North Adams is thirsty for Pym housewares. They enhance their quality of life and help them feel a bit more affluent. The Adams brothers sell out soon after they're delivered. CJ and I consider ourselves lucky to have acquired several pieces for our apartment on the second floor of the Colgrove Building. When we asked Mr. Adams how he could charge so little for such quality furniture, he told us Jubal simply refuses to charge more because the Pyms consider money the root of all evil and only need funds sufficient to support Notchboro.

So, what's going on with Freddie? In just about every sense, he's a Pym: tall, strapping ... but today when we got a close look, it became apparent that something wasn't quite right. His eyes were dull. His countenance projected confusion rather than guile. Freddie's body posture was uncertain and shy. And then I remembered something Father Lynch had mentioned in passing,

"... butt of jokes on every trip to the village. Tormented."

And then ... unable to be unable to talk? I can't imagine!

Still, Freddie never showed anger or hostility toward anyone. A normal person would build up a rage. But wasn't that the crux of the case, now? Not what a normal person might feel or do, but what *Freddie* actually felt and was capable of. Did Terence and Jasper box him into a corner, so he believed he was fighting to survive? Or was Freddie's response to their aggressive approach simply the second violent expression of a mind which had already crossed the line by murdering Shayleigh Grogan two nights before? To my mind, there was only one way to be sure ...

Find a way to get close to him. Touch him if I can. The answer is in his heart.

This thought had no sooner crossed my mind than Jubal was headed back out to speak with Da. When he reached the gateway of the cemetery, the clansmen flowed back, surrounding Freddie, protecting him. Now lost to our view, it was as if his soul had been reclaimed the sea.

"I could have tol' you 'bout Freddie, but I don't think you'd 've believed me, Cap'n. The fact is, Freddie's a child; a very large, very trusting child. Wouldn't hurt a fly unless he was most grievously provoked. The Ingersolls must've done been 'special cruel for him to lash out the way he did. And t' answer your next question; he certainly doesn't lust after women."

Jubal paused for a moment, looked down at the ground while he toed the soil, and moaned,

"You see, Elder Cyrus castrates our mooncalves soon as they show signs of the change."

Clearly dismayed by this revelation, Jubal inhaled deeply before somberly carrying on,

"Freddie's not the first ... and he won't be the last."

Finally, Jubal grumbled,

"It's how we protect the clan."

What?

I was so shocked that I turned and stormed from the scene, lest I spew the words which might allow me to vent my disgust but in the end change nothing. According to Cyrus and Jubal, gelding those damaged was the clan's way and that's all there was to it.

Holy Saints Patrick, Brigit and Colmcille! What else might these people be capable of?

Puzzlement, befuddlement and disenchantment accompanied CJ and me on our ride back to Constable Station. From the moment I arrived in Notchboro, wonder had escalated only to be dashed into stupefaction. And I didn't at'all like the conflicting thoughts now swimming in my head.

The charming maze of cottages we passed on our way up to the Pym's cemetery became a shantytown of tired shacks upon our return. The path that had earlier led us from the dimness of the forest canopy toward a sunlit field was less than treacherous, but a bit slippery, nonetheless. Mud covered Da's boots and clung to the hem of Father Lynch's cassock. The ethereal mist emanating from the sawmill's water wheel now simply rained uncomfortably down upon us.

The serene village of Notchboro became the symbol of a cloistered society pure in its intent but perverted in its expression.

The Pyms didn't just shun society; they threatened outsiders with physical harm and possible death for intruding into territory they'd claimed as their own. These people lived in isolation by choice, courted and married only each other. And when their incest caused things to go horribly wrong, the error was stopped in its tracks by mutilating the innocent result.

Once we returned to civilization and were riding side by side down Witt Avenue, Conal said,

"I do confess, Virginia, when I mentioned the Pyms had their ways, I had no idea ... Can I assume you know what castrate means?"

CJ had spoken up just as my disgust and anger reached its crescendo. So naturally my ire directed itself at my beloved, and I responded with dripping sarcasm,

"Can I assume you remember I grew up on a farm?"

Immediately regretful, I attempted reclamation,

"Oh, CJ, forgive me! I'm just so appalled with the whole lot of them. What a sick, sick society. It's hard enough to understand why they live the way they do; harder still to understand how they could mutilate one of their own as they did."

Ignoring my insult, CJ's smile expressed tenderness, but his eyes displayed our shared consternation.

"I agree. But remember, this trip wasn't about cultural analysis. Nor was it within our purview to moralize about the Pyms. We went for one reason: to determine whether Freddie Pym could throttle a vulnerable young woman to near unconsciousness before raping her. Then, once he could inflict no further terror, he not only murdered Shayleigh Grogan but also had the presence of mind while on his way home to dispose of the trash by tossing her off Witt's Ledge."

Of course, CJ was right. This was the act of a cold, calculating predator. I certainly didn't need to interact with Freddie Pym's soul to conclude that even if he were whole and capable of doing any *one* of the things CJ had mentioned, there was simply no way he could string together the series in a premeditated way. Add to that the effects of being gelded ...

Yes, If I were Freddie, I'd commit murder, alright. And toss the trash off a cliff, too. But the victim would be Elder --- Cyrus --- Pym. But first I'd get a dull knife and cut off his ...

Virginia Daelyn!!!

Startled back to reality from my own dark thoughts and emotions, or had it been Seanmháthair? I asked,

"So, what do we do now?"

CJ chuckled and nodding his head forward began,

"Well, Virginia, the first thing we need to do ..."

Then, timing the moment I looked away, CJ spurred Killian to a sprint and called out over his shoulder,

"... is catch-up with the rest of the group."

Aaaggghhh ... you bloody gobshite!!

Chapter 14

A New Consideration

By the time we'd all arrived back in the village it was nearly dark. We were tired, hungry, and even though only Doc could hear it, the Wilson House saloon beckoned. Father Lynch accepted Doc's invitation to join him in a libation or two before dinner, but Da simply chuckled and waved Doc off.

"Thanks, Doc, but Maeve 'll hold supper just so long before it becomes a cannonade and I end up wearing it, rather than eating it. As it is ..."

The intent of Da's pause became obvious when he turned to face us; he wanted our company just in case.

"Sorry, Da, but CJ and I have plans."

Da smirked knowingly as he nudged Rusty homeward, waved goodbye, and said,

"It was worth a try."

Once the Captain was out of earshot, CJ raised an eyebrow as he asked,

"And what plans would those be, you devious divil?"

I turned my head askew knowingly and smirked, but otherwise ignored Conal's intent and continued,

"By now you should know as well as I that Da has a much better chance of eating his supper rather than wearing it if he comes home alone. He can slump his shoulders, drag his feet ... Get the picture?"

Having partaken of a most satisfactory meal of Irish stew and a pint or two at the Old Black Tavern, CJ and I entered the back door of the Colgrove Block only to find bright light seeping down the corridor leading from Jeremiah's office. We were both taken aback because Jeremiah never worked after supper. Time and again he'd chased *us* out of the office promptly at six o'clock saying, "What good is money if you have no time to spend it? Now, get!"

There could only be one possible reason he remained here into the night. It must have been obvious to CJ, as well, because he winced at me as he whispered,

"I'm pretty tired. Do we really want to do this tonight? If we close the door quietly, I'll bet we can get upstairs without Jeremiah hearing."

I copied CJ's tone as I replied,

"It's not going to go away, Conal. Besides, we both know *he'll* know. C'mon."

I reached back, and squeezing CJ's hand added,

"It'll be alright. By the way, do you speak Latin?"

CJ purposefully closed the door to cover his nervous titter and said,

"That's for you two, Ginger. I'm not quite part of *that* club yet. I think for now I'll stick to English. Besides, since when are we afraid of Jeremiah Colgrove ... Right?"

CJ had no sooner shot me an imploring glance than Jeremiah's door opened, and we were challenged to answer that question.

Ever imperious, ever impeccable, there stood himself nearly filling the doorway.

Or was he?

It was upon second glance I noticed how expectations had altered my perception. Jeremiah's waistcoat was unbuttoned, and his ascot loosened to reveal an opened top shirt button. That was all. But it was enough. These were two more things Jeremiah Colgrove III simply never did. Furthermore, the hands which reached up and clutched the top door casing did not bring to mind Atlas supporting the weight of the world, but instead a haggard Anyman hanging on to survive it.

In all my life I'd never seen my friend daunted in any way, let alone discomfited. Impulsively, I ran the length of the corridor and embraced him. Behind me CJ exclaimed,

"My gosh, Jer, what in blazes has happened?"

Jeremiah's answer was to shed my embrace without returning it, purse his lips, and with a sweep of his left arm beckon us into his office. Crossing the threshold didn't allay our perplexity either, because despite Jeremiah's appearance, everything seemed normal. His desk was as neat as a pin. His suit jacket was draped over the back of his desk chair. Clients' chairs were tidily arranged in front of his desk and unpopulated. The only hint that something *was* amiss occupied the Chesterfield set against the office wall to our right. There, in all his glory, was the recumbent figure of Jeremiah Colgrove II, Jeremiah's father.

However, the ever-jovial pater Colgrove popped in so often during the week for what he regarded as, "a stopover, a snort and a snooze," that the real warning bells only rang in my head when I beheld his blank, detached countenance.

It was only when Jeremiah announced our arrival that he rolled over and stood up to greet us. Mr. Colgrove's smile was forced and at best wanly offered.

"Thank you for coming," was all he said.

Victorian decorum served, Jeremiah's father nodded, turned away, and hands clasped behind him proceeded to the window behind Jeremiah's desk where he gazed out at the nothing to be seen on the other side. During the ensuing silence, I couldn't help but notice how very much the two Jeremiahs resembled one another. Over six feet tall and exceedingly handsome, both would appear patrician dressed in workman's clothes and boots. Only the hints of silver streaking through the elder's hair and the closely cropped Van Dyke surrounding his mouth separated them.

Just then, I was drawn back from my thoughts as the silence was interrupted:

"Shayleigh Grogan worked as a spinner at Pater's cotton mill. He knew her name but didn't realize she was the girl who'd lost her life until this morning when she was reported missing from work."

Jeremiah paused as he walked around behind us and closed his office door before continuing in almost a whisper,

"But he did ... *know* her."

Hearing *this* jolted me as if I'd been struck by lightning. Shayleigh's vacant eyes demanding I experience her terror, and the despondency of her impending death roared back. But as I strove to vault from my chair, CJ squeezed my hand with one of his and reached across to restrain me with his other. When I turned my head to question his action, the look of calm I beheld on his face deflated me, and I melted back into my chair. Then, CJ added,

"Why don't you continue, Jer? Tell us what you mean by *know ...*"

Jeremiah moved behind his desk and matching my actions, he too collapsed unceremoniously into his chair. He leaned back and folded his hands under his chin as if preparing to pray. Closing his eyes, he inhaled deeply seeming to steel himself for what he was about to say. However, all this took time; time Jeremiah's pater was evidently unwilling to waste.

"Never mind son," Jeremiah's father smoldered as he turned back to face us, "I've got this."

Now standing next to Jeremiah, Pater touched his son's shoulder gently with the flat of his hand before continuing sternly,

"Yes, I knew her. But all I tried to do was help!"

Hesitating for a second to calm himself and collect his thoughts, Mr. Colgrove continued,

"Some of the girls at the mill are married and have children who also work there. A few of the husbands work at the mill, as well. Unmarried girls often come off the farms while still in their teens hoping to find husbands. Others because their family farms have failed and can no longer support them."

"Immigrants arriving on our shores every day are forced to diffuse from the congestion, meanness and violence of the cities. This sort come and go constantly, and never remain past their early twenties."

"Regardless, there is a palpable hardiness about all of them ... a determined nature helping them to survive. A few even flourish in the mills, becoming unofficial leaders of their shifts ... the sort other workers look up to even more than their appointed supervisors."

"Shayleigh was none of these. She may have worked at the mill, but she was never part of its community. And because of that," Pater counted off on his fingers as he continued, "she ate alone, sat alone on breaks, and walked home from work unaccompanied."

"Most of the year that's perfectly safe. But now it's autumn, near dark by the end of the workday, and because of that quite a foolhardy undertaking. So, whenever I saw Shayleigh alone while heading down Marshall Street on her way toward the River Street row houses, I'd invite her to join me in my carriage."

"BUT THAT WAS ALL!" Mr. Colgrove barked.

Rising from his chair, Jeremiah took over,

"But that's not how it looks. Let's examine the circumstances, counselors: Pater had direct contact with the victim. While it has not been established that father invited Miss Grogan to ride in his carriage on the night of her murder, his invitations had been observed frequently enough to imply familiarity. Next, the method of Shayleigh's murder required physical strength, a cold calculating mind and ... and ... I'm sorry, father ... a certain ruthlessness. Again, all true. And finally, the mill's wags have been spreading poison about how they believed Pater *knew* Miss Grogan for quite a while. The Captain will surely find out this information soon enough. So, you tell me, CJ, what will he do when he does?"

"After all, it's no secret that the Captain bears only a grudging acceptance that my father even exists. Pater is a mill owner and, therefore, in his eyes a predator who promises a better life, but instead works village families and vulnerable immigrants nearly to death in the name of profit."

Jeremiah paused, inhaled deeply and puffing his lips while exhaling through tightly held lips resumed...

"And so, I'll ask ... no, I'll plead for your help. You see, the foundation of my reticence is not Pater's relationship with Shayleigh Grogan. It's because I must ask the unaskable ... for you, Ginger, and CJ to intercede on behalf of my father ... to protect him from the Captain."

I could sense this coming. This whole scene had been a contrivance which unfolded too predictably to not end as it did. This was exactly the way Jeremiah operated. CJ and I had been craftily manipulated into a corner, and neither Colgrove cared a bit about the strain exerted upon our relationships.

So, flabbergasted was the wrong word to describe my response, though I'm quite sure my countenance might have said so. A year ago, I would have exploded at the insult of being used in this way ... that he could believe I was so stupid I wouldn't notice. But today I had come to accept that not even his best friends were immune to Jeremiah's situational ethics, or what he might do because of them. He knew we knew what he was doing. He simply didn't care. He'd done it before. And if he rationalized the need, would do it again. It was simply part of the price one paid for being Jeremiah Colgrove's friend.

So, CJ and I were polite, but very careful to make no commitment to either of the Jeremiahs. As expected, my Jeremiah displayed consternation, feigning an inability to understand why we should feel so put out. Just as predictably, my hackles rose as I'd finally had enough, and prepared to pounce. Mercifully, CJ was there, and in one smooth action thrust an admonishing finger to pursed lips, freezing me in my tracks. Then he swung around to blazon that look of exasperation Jeremiah had come to respect and learned to heed.

"Jeremiah, the Captain never has, and never will, run roughshod over *anyone* in the pursuit of justice. That your father and Captain O'Leary don't see eye to eye is irrelevant."

CJ then paused as he faced Jeremiah's father.

"Now, sir, Virginia and I will convey your message of admitted involvement in this matter ... and that it was freely given. What we will *not* do is to personalize the matter. This comes down to a question of trust in the integrity and humanity of the Captain."

And me Da will need to trust that you meant no insult to either his intelligence or sensitivity to your business position.

At that, CJ took me by the arm and, allowing no opportunity for discussion or rebuttal, we quit the scene and fled for our apartment upstairs.

It's surprising how exhaustion is incapable of preventing sleeplessness when a person is confronted by a no-win situation. Over and over I turned. Over and over I replayed the scene in Jeremiah's office. I knew what CJ said we'd do ... and how Da would respond. What was left unsaid was that I was also sure Da would demand to know what side we were on.

And right now, I didn't know the answer to that question.

Chapter 15
One Man's Consideration …

As things turned out, Da never asked. Instead he simply leaned back as far as the groaning springs of his desk chair would allow and interlocking his fingers behind his head smiled wryly at the two of us.

"Must be a terrible life, bein' a Colgrove. Just terrible. Richer than Midas, they are, and knowin' there's a world out there, conspiring all day, every day t' take it'all away."

At that, Da leaned forward, jutted his chin forward before derisively whispering,

"And because of that they trust no one. The problem with that is their attitude shows through. Their arrogance alienates those few folks who *do* stand ready t' offer assistance."

Da closed his eyes for a second, pausing. When he opened them, he was looking at the ceiling and curtly shook his head back and forth like he couldn't believe what he was about to say:

"Anyhow, I'll take a long, deep breath and give 'em a pass. The bloody eejits simply can't help themselves. 'Tis a shame it never occurred to them that they both have actually earned my respect for *how* they survive in their world."

When I turned to CJ with a start, Da rose from his chair, glared at CJ and me and growled,

"'Tis better you see what I mean for yourselves. Now, get on with it! Get over to that mill. I'm sure the world that really does wish the Colgroves harm is getting wind of the situation even as we speak. And right now that means I'm caught in the middle."

Then the Captain walked to his office door, opened it and with a casual sweep of his arm invited us to leave.

"I'm too young to retire to the farm ... and too old t' have a boss ... especially when that boss 'll be your Ma!"

It was just after ten in the morning when CJ and I crossed from the western reaches of Center Street to the far side of the contrariwise running Marshall and arrived at the front gate of the *Adams North Village Cotton and Woolen Manufacturing Company*. The gate keeper was an older man, gray of hair, but impeccable of dress. Rising from his chair to greet us, he nodded and stood proudly, but winced with each step he took. As he reached out to unlatch the wrought iron gate his right hand revealed stumps where his first three fingers should have been.

When I looked quizzically at CJ and nodded at the deformity, the man ignored me and simply smiled,

"'Morning, folks and welcome. My name's George. What's your business this fine day?"

CJ introduced both of us and inquired if Mr. Colgrove had a few minutes to see us. George merely nodded, waved us both in, and secured the gate as we proceeded on our way. Once we were out of earshot I quietly whispered to CJ,

"Well, what do you make of George? Was he a soldier with you in the 27th Massachusetts?"

CJ chuckled at my question, so I bopped his arm a good one before he could respond,

"George is *just* a bit along to have gallivanted through the Carolina woods taking part in our hit and run operations. But you *have* seen injuries like these before."

It was only a moment before I flashed upon the scenes I'd so often beheld in the Old Black Tavern. Men stooped and broken. Twisted legs that had been left unset to heal the best way they could. Fingers and sometimes hands missing. Surly, despondent men. Men existing in an alcoholic haze, biding their time until they died.

But this wasn't George. Sure, he was maimed. He was nagged by persistent pain. But George had a job. He was proud. He had self-respect.

And I was confused.

It was only a short distance farther along the gravel walkway to reach the granite block and mortar two-storey box which was the mill. The front face was barely seventy-five feet across. Both floors were illuminated by large multi-paned windows glaring back at us as they reflected the morning sun. As we approached, my ears began to ring when they detected an almost subliminal droning hum coming from the mill. Double-doors were painted bright green, located on the left side, and surprisingly small given they looked to be the only way in or out for its many workers, as well as the mill's raw materials. To the right of the door was a tarnished brass plaque which caused CJ and me to pause. It proclaimed that this indeed was *the Adams North Cotton and Woolen Manufacturing Company*, founded in 1810 by Captain Jeremiah Colgrove, Benjamin Sibley and Josh Waterman. My gosh, that was our Jeremiah's grandfather! When I reached out and traced the raised letters on the plaque, I went weak in the knees and suddenly Jeremiah and I were at the Colgrove manse.

We couldn't have been more than seven or eight years old. He had tugged on my plait in retaliation after I'd stuck out my tongue at him for ... who knows what. Anyhow, I was chasing Jeremiah down the service corridor, into the dining room, through the parlor, across the vestibule until finally Jeremiah scooted into the turret room his father used for his home office. When I crossed the threshold and was about to pounce on him as he cowered under his father's desk, I suddenly balked. Staring down at me from the wall, frozen in time by oil paint, and framed in gold, a stern face demanded my attention.

I nearly jumped out of my skin when a man's voice behind me said,

"The Captain had that effect on everyone."

Jeremiah smiled and popped his head above the desk and called out,

"Pater!"

I turned, was confronted by the reincarnation of the man in the painting and found myself only slightly relieved. But Jeremiah Colgrove II beamed at both of us. It was just like him to not scold us for being in his office, but make his point, nonetheless.

Then it was suddenly 1866 again and my husband was standing beside me. I had no idea how long I winked out this time, but I was back. It must have been the cacophony funneling through the doorway CJ had just opened that did the trick. I found myself a bit disoriented by the racket, but nonetheless undaunted I shouted,

"CJ, I think I get it. It'all makes sense!"

CJ, who had certainly seen me get "that look" and drift off so often before, merely shrugged quizzically, shook his head, and pointed to his ears. Frustrated by how little CJ seemed to be moved by my enthusiasm, I stormed past him and through the doorway.

My story would need to wait.

Chapter 16
Beasts of Burden

Once inside, my consternation quickly faded away as we found ourselves engulfed by droning sounds which caused my head to thud in cadence with the mill's operation. The atmosphere was clammy and thick enough with dust to tickle my nose. With each breath it caused me to clear my already irritated throat. The cavernous room which loomed before us was nearly as long as the seventy-five-foot width of the building's front face. It was hard to estimate the ceiling's height, but when I looked up two rows of windows were visible. In addition, the ceiling which began just above them continued, following the roof's steep slope to the peak.

The sources of the din commanded the complete attention of several men whose sole job seemed to be the feeding and care of the two mechanical beasts before us. Huge burlap-wrapped bales of raw cotton lined up three deep along the wall were in the process of being unwrapped by workers and shoved one by one into the maw of the first machine. As they were devoured, fuzzy dust and dirt was spat everywhere, while bats of loose, fluffy cotton were ejected from its backside.

Another crew of workers hurriedly gathered up the discharged bats and fed them into the hopper of the next machine. From it, a continuous flimsy sheet of grayish matting emerged which was rolled and cut off at what seemed to be a predetermined girth. Once released, another group of men grunted with the strain of catching the heavy loads and stacking them on a dolly. These finished products of the room's travail were then muscled up a half-level and through a large doorway to feed whatever processes were being performed on the other side.

Directly to our left, a small set of stairs led to another green door which beckoned us to discover what those processes might be. Once we'd crossed through, I found myself gaping at a room which dwarfed the one we'd just left. While it may have been the same width, it was easily twice that in length, and maybe a bit more. There were plenty of windows to brighten the space. However, the mid-morning sun was largely shut out by a grayish film which covered panes of glass made pasty by rivulets of condensation running down them. A steamy mist hovering over the entire space further scattered any surviving light rays into a shadowy dusk.

Anchored to crossbeams high above us, a spider's web of iron shafts and pulleys whirred as they connected leather belts to long lines of the extraordinary machines they powered. The constant clacks, whines and whirs, while not as loud as the opening room, seemed able to produce a charged atmosphere that made my hair stand on end.

Yellowed letters painted on the wall to our right spelling out "OFFICE" directed us to climb a steep set of stairs which led to a second-floor landing and a room-sized rectangular wooden box suspended from the roof crossbeams. We'd only climbed about halfway when the reasons for the precarious position of our destination dawned on me. With each riser we conquered, noises diminished, and the air cleared. When I glanced to my left, operations of the entire mill played out before my eyes.

Upon reaching the platform and opening the office door, a reserved young man wearing a starched white shirt and wide cravat looked up from the papers strewn before him on his desk. No greeting was offered and the look on his face made it quite clear our presence was not appreciated. Thankfully, we'd no sooner introduced ourselves than Jeremiah's father appeared at the doorway of his office and invited us to come in. He closed the door behind us, and as we all took a seat he asked,

"Is this a pleasant surprise, or should I get my hat and coat?"

Ah, the Colgrove charm. In one short sentence, Mr. Colgrove both disarmed us and got to the point.

It was CJ who spoke next:

"No, sir, I'm not here to arrest you or even to ask you to come along. In fact, I can't because, technically, I'm no longer employed by the village constabulary. However, the Captain *did* send us. His concern is not that you had anything to do with Shayleigh Grogan's murder; it's that your enemies will seize upon the opportunity to turn public opinion in that direction ... And the clock is ticking."

Mr. Colgrove stood, turned to look out his office window and asked,

"Do I have you and Virginia to thank for interceding on my behalf?"

Hearing that made me bristle,

"No, sir!"

No sooner had I blurted that out than I caught myself and remembered that none of the Colgroves seem able to help themselves. In their minds, advantage and entitlement were their due. So, I took a calming breath and quietly continued,

"You sell yourself short, sir. And if you believe that anything I or Conal could say would change the way the Captain enforces the law ... well, you've sold him short as well. The fact is, my Da believes you to be an honorable man. And it's because of the good will you've earned with him that you're not sitting in a cell right now."

Far from offended, Mr. Colgrove chuckled as he turned back to face both CJ and me and said,

"And I hope to never do anything to alter his opinion, Ginger. Thank you for making that clear."

With that simple sign of gratitude, the tension in the room evaporated. Mr. Colgrove crossed his arms and smiled broadly at the two of us and asked,

"So, what's next?"

Chapter 17
(Smaller) Beasts of Burden

After it had been decided that talking to Shayleigh's coworkers was a good place to start, Mr. Colgrove led us outside of the office and onto the stair landing. Leaning casually forward, he rested both elbows on the railing as he began,

"At first glance I'm sure things going on below look more than a bit convoluted. But think of it this way. All we do is turn bales of cotton it into thread and then we weave it into fabric. When you folks came in you saw the first steps in the process. Shayleigh Grogan was a spinner, which is the last step in thread making. In this mill we have three spinning machines, one in each of the rows before us."

Then Mr. Colgrove straightened up and pointing into the distance with his right index finger continued,

Shayleigh's spinning machine is ... um, *was* in the right row about half-way down. It's the long machine that looks like a hundred strands of yarn are feeding into it. Very difficult to operate because strands break all the time and need to be mended together quickly or the spinner clogs up shutting everything down, sometimes for hours. All those bobbins collecting the spun thread need to be monitored closely as well. Once full, they need to be removed and replaced immediately or the overflow strands will also clog up the works."

Pater then turned back to face us and hugging himself tightly closed his eyes. The vision he saw in his mind's eye caused him to wince, and he took a deep collecting breath before he continued,

"And they're quite dangerous too, as I'm sure you can imagine. All those moving parts ... fingers ... hair ... and sometimes even clothing become snagged in the machinery. Injuries don't happen often, but when they do the results can be horrendous."

At that, Jeremiah's father paused and the three of us shared an impromptu moment of quiet, reflecting upon the reality of working in a textile mill.

"Anyhow, Jeff Corbin's the man you should start with. He oversees the spinning operation and can answer your questions. You can't miss him because he's in constant motion ... Oh, and he's got only one arm."

Without further explanation Mr. Colgrove walked back into the office and quietly closed the door.

As CJ and I walked along one of the alleyways created by the rows of machines, Mr. Colgrove's admonishments kept us mindful to stay clear of all moving parts as well as to not interfere with the men and women operating them. In addition, thanks to him, the purpose of each machine became logical and easy to track.

The first machines we encountered were fed sheets of cotton we'd seen produced in the opening room and run through rollers covered with tiny wire pins. The sheets were then shredded, and the longer fibers channeled into funnels. But lint and dust from this operation were also flying everywhere and seemed to float in the atmosphere until it all settled out in the back of my throat. If it was possible, the air near *these* machines was even worse than the opening room.

Fuzzy cotton ropes emerged from the bottom of the funnels which then loosely pirouetted into collecting cans. Each succeeding machine we passed stretched, twisted and refined these cotton ropes a bit more until a fine yarn was produced. The spinning machines further twisted, stretched and wound the yarn into thread, finalizing the process.

It was also obvious that as the cotton became more and more refined, the skills required to operate the machines did too. And so, by the time we reached the spinning machines, women completely displaced men as the sole operators.

What we weren't prepared for was the heat generated by the machines which seemed to evaporate the moisture running down the film-covered windows producing a haze that enveloped us, only to re-condense when it contacted the cold concrete floors. The overall result was an atmosphere so stiflingly hot and thick with dust you could cut it with a knife, and floors so cold and slimy on your feet you felt you were ice skating with every step. Given the circumstances, the staccato periodic hacking which managed to penetrate the constant din was far from surprising to hear.

However, the biggest surprise was reserved for our arrival at the spinning machines. Not just because the women operators seemed able to flawlessly keep track of nearly a hundred separate spinners, but because they were also supervising children who seemed to be everywhere! Some as young as six, others as old as ten. And none were there to play. A few used mops bigger than they were to swab the slimy floors as dry as possible. Still others nimbly climbed barefooted all over the spinning machines changing out empty bobbins for full ones!

I immediately felt myself become tense with dread. These children seemed completely oblivious to the dangers of the spinning, whirling, wracking motions of machines only inches away which seemed hungry to gobble them up. I concluded that each of them must have been protected by their own personal guardian angel. So intently was I focused that I visibly shuddered when CJ brushed my cheek with his as he called directly into my ear,

"Would you mind releasing my hand? You're breaking it!"

I looked down to see that, indeed, our hand-holding which began as a way to protect one another as we negotiated this dangerous gauntlet had progressed to Conal's fingers being squashed in my vise-like grip. I winced in sympathy to my husband's discomfort, released his hand and returned,

"Can you believe this place? My God!"

The faint smile he offered was full of compassion and sighed,

"The children. It's always the children who have it the worst."

As he turned back to watch them, I knew there was more he almost said, but didn't ... and wouldn't.

"Stand right there!" a gruff voice commanded and then continued, "What in the name of custard are you two doing here?"

Almost immediately, a mountain of a man whose right arm ended at his elbow appeared from around the far side of the spinning machines and glared at the both of us. Muscular and easily as tall as I, his hair was close cropped, his expression severe. There was no question; this was the man in charge. And this was a man who felt very comfortable waiting for an answer.

So Conal gave him one:

"Mr. Corbin? My name is Conal Mulcahy and this is Virginia."

When his answer made absolutely no impression on the supervisor, CJ added,

"Mr. Colgrove said it would be alright for us to come down here and have a talk with you."

CJ paused allowing that to sink in, but Corbin flatly said,

"Colgrove may own this mill, but he don't run these machines ... and he don't tell me who I gotta' talk to either."

At that he walked away from us and over his shoulder barked,

"You found your way in ... you can find your way out."

CJ's brow furrowed. He'd had just about enough and was about to make a fuss, so I quickly called out,

"We're in charge of finding out who murdered Shayleigh Grogan."

Corbin stopped cold in his tracks. His shoulders slumped and he grumbled,

"Murdered?"

Then turning to face us he roared,

"I knew it! I told everyone they was wrong!"

At that he bolted off along the corridor leading out and screamed,

"I'll kill him! That son of a bitch ... dallying with her, pickin' her up in that fancy carriage of his and takin' her God knows where..."

It was when he mentioned the carriage that we connected just who the focus of Corbin's rage was, and where he was going. CJ and I immediately gave chase, and together we tackled Corbin at the bottom of the office stairs. Even so, he was so strong he managed to stand back up with the two of us riding him. Unable to shrug us off, Corbin started to climb, but found himself looking down the barrel of a Sharps carbine held by Mr. Colgrove's secretary. Only the click-click of the hammer being cocked stopped Corbin.

The total time of the tussle couldn't have been longer than a minute or so. Nevertheless, Mr. Colgrove had already arrived on the stair landing and was looking down upon the mess.

"Let him go." He called to CJ and me.

"And for heaven's sake, Poole, stand that weapon down!"

Poole called over his shoulder, "I don't think that's a very good idea, sir."

"Do it!" Mr. Colgrove barked.

CJ and I slid off Corbin's back and landed a stair below as Poole pointed the rifle toward the ceiling, and using his thumb controlled the hammer's release. Confused, but still furious, Jeff Corbin stood transfixed and huffed loudly as he glared up at Jeremiah's father. Undaunted, Mr. Colgrove proceeded to descend the stairs until he came face to face with his nemesis, and staring him down almost whispered,

"Mr. Corbin, do you hate me so much that the truth no longer matters to you?"

Mr. Colgrove then turned his back on him and heading back up the stairs called out,

"Well, Mr. Corbin, are you coming?"

Chapter 18
An Introspection

While Mr. Colgrove's office had seemed cramped when three of us were there the first time, at least some relief was provided by a window which looked out upon the Hoosic River's north branch as it made its final rush through the village from the mountains of Vermont. Windows or not, however, the addition of a sullen and openly hostile Jeff Corbin leaning back against the closed door created a feeling of entrapment that caused CJ and me to sit sideways in our chairs so we could track his every movement. Mr. Colgrove, on the other hand, stood unconcerned with his back to all of us looking out the window. There was only a short pause before he quietly but forcefully said,

"Mr. Corbin, I'm sorry you blame me for the loss of your arm. I'm sorry you will never appreciate my efforts to make amends. So, I'll not attempt to explain why Miss Grogan's death has cut me as deeply as it has you."

Mr. Colgrove then turned to face us, leaned forward over his desk, and bracing himself by extended arms continued,

"But I *will* ask you to talk to Sergeant Mulcahy and Miss Virginia. You know who they are, and you also know they've been sent by Constable Captain O'Leary."

And then, the strain from a sleepless night clearly apparent, Mr. Colgrove seemed to plead,

"The question is, Jeff, will you help them?"

At that, Mr. Colgrove worked his way around his desk and by CJ and me. He brushed Corbin out of the way with a withering glare and opened the office door. Then turning back to look at each of us, he seemed on the verge of saying something but instead walked out of the office without further comment and firmly closed the door.

CJ and I looked at each other hoping we didn't betray the discomfiture we so obviously felt at Mr. Colgrove's departure. After all, it was only a few minutes ago that Jeff Corbin had proven himself capable of murdering Jeremiah's father, even while carrying CJ and me on his back. Only a cocked rifle pointed between his eyes had dissuaded him. That single display of blood lust established that while Jeff Corbin may have been missing part of his right arm, he was certainly more than capable of restraining, raping and doing away with the slight and demure Shayleigh Grogan.

It also vaulted Corbin to the front of the line as a prime suspect. For, while Jeremiah's father circumstantially fit the bill, I'd never in all my life seen him display the rage that seemed to come so naturally to Jeff Corbin. In fact, I'd never seen him lose his temper in *any* way. And it was that quality which made him such an exasperating business rival. Logic always trumped emotion.

However, when I stole a quick glance at Corbin, his shoulders were slumped, his eyes downcast. The man before us showed all the signs of remorse and sadness, but I couldn't be sure what his despondency was about.

Time to find out!

So, I said,

"Pardon my abruptness, Mr. Corbin, but you, sir, are a jackass!"

At that, I thought I heard CJ nearly gag. Then CJ moaned,

"Ginger, for heaven's sake don't provoke him."

Now, I know my beloved's concern was that he was all that stood between Corbin and me, should he again erupt, but I sensed no danger emanating from this man. In fact, I was more than a bit surprised that his aura displayed not one hint of the evil I know I sensed around me for a moment during the scuffle at the base of the stairs. Nevertheless, I quickly winked at CJ with the eye Corbin couldn't see and then continued,

"The way I see it, life has done you dirt, sure. But you're far from alone. The saloons and cemeteries of the village are populated with others just like you. They've been discarded and forgotten. However, Mr. Colgrove saw something in you, and has not only kept you employed; he has also put you in a position of charge to see that others aren't befallen by your fate."

At that, Corbin raised his eyes and met mine. But this time his glare fell short of the hostility of our first meeting. So, I rushed on,

"Yet your hatred of Mr. Colgrove continues to cross the line."

When no answer was forthcoming, I stood up and maneuvered my way to the only other office window. It looked out upon the production floor below and as I surveyed the scene before me, I beheld Mr. Colgrove in the distance assisting a young woman who was somewhat clumsily learning to operate Shayleigh Grogan's spinning machine. I then called over my shoulder while nodding toward the window,

"So, Mr. Corbin, this is the man you hate so?"

When he took a step toward me, CJ bolted from his chair interjecting himself between Corbin and me as they both approached the window. However, it was only as we three evaluated the scene below that I was reminded that perspective is so often based upon our personal biases. While I witnessed a benevolent adult teaching a young woman, Corbin …

"He's at it again! Watch the lecher! In a minute he'll have his hands all over her!"

It was then a little birdie whispered in my ear,

"Nice try, Ginger, why don't you let me take it from here."

The birdie was Conal. And at this point I was more than happy to relinquish the floor. The way I was going, Mr. Poole was going to need his carbine again!

"Mr. Corbin," CJ began, "we're here to listen and learn. Our purpose is solely to find the truth. Every scrap of information is important to us. But all I've seen thus far is a man I know to be fair and honest attacked by you, treated with disdain and hatred. And instead of seeing you at this moment locked in a cell or at least turned out onto the street, Mr. Colgrove has chosen to do your job while you talk to us. You'll go home a free man this evening, Mr. Corbin, with a full day's pay."

Then, grabbing Corbin's arm, CJ turned him, so they were face to face.

"Now, please … tell me why I'm wrong."

For the next half-hour I stood back, and for once in my life kept quiet, as CJ skillfully drew information out of Jeff Corbin. He'd challenged Corbin to explain why he interpreted the scene below so differently. And the combative Corbin almost gleefully took the bait.

He did, in fact, blame Mr. Colgrove for the loss of his arm. Much of his identity was wrapped up in his physical strength. So, on that fateful day when he attempted to unclog the opening machine he worked on and reached in too far … Jeff Corbin's world changed forever. He'd survived the amputation, the fever, the long healing process. And after all of this, his right hand and forearm were gone, and only the stump remained. He aimlessly wandered about Main Street for months with nothing to do and no prospects for future employment. And in his mind, it was Colgrove's machine that had taken everything away.

Even after Mr. Poole had knocked on the door of Corbin's house bearing news that Mr. Colgrove would not only pay his medical bills, but also guarantee him a better job than the one he had before, Corbin still returned to the mill with a chip on his shoulder. And it was that attitude which colored everything. The fact that Mr. Colgrove never once solicited appreciation mattered little to Corbin because it was an apology for what had happened to him Corbin craved … not master to servant, but man to man.

It became clear to CJ and me that in Corbin's eyes Mr. Colgrove could do no right. In addition, Corbin was self-conscious of his debility and extremely sensitive how the other men saw him. He felt they saw him as less than a man, and so he saw himself that way. Once he started his new job as spinning supervisor, Corbin bristled at Mr. Colgrove's visits to the production floor. He saw every kindness or expression of concern as an unwanted advance by a rich, powerful man upon him … his sisters … his children. Every gentle or friendly touch was deemed as lechery. Mr. Colgrove's treatment of workers as fellow human beings and equals was perceived to be insincere condescension.

When CJ continued to probe, Corbin admitted that Mr. Colgrove treated everyone this way, but for reasons he was wont to explain, still saw Pater's treatment of Shayleigh as different, threatening. However, it was also apparent to me that Jeff Corbin was such a successful foreman because of the pain he'd endured and harbored an almost pathological fear for the safety of the women and children he supervised. That translated into a fraternal love for his people and a deep need to protect them ... especially from the likes of Jeremiah Colgrove II, owner-operator of *The Adams North Cotton and Woolen Manufacturing Company*.

That realization hit me hard. Jeff Corbin was no murderer. While he may have been an overly sensitive man easily slighted, he was also a caring, good hearted man who saw Shayleigh Grogan as an especially fragile, vulnerable young woman in need of protection. Indeed, it was his failure to protect her that triggered his violent response. The irony was, Jeff Corbin and Jeremiah Colgrove should have been fast friends, not adversaries. When I noticed Corbin's demeanor again slump, I couldn't help but believe this same thought might have just crossed his mind. And once again I couldn't help but blurt out,

"Mr. Corbin. You sir, really *are* a jackass."

Chapter 19
Her Favorite Little Doffer

CJ noticed the change in Corbin's demeanor as well, and this time requested rather than challenged his assistance. Corbin's only response was a quick nod followed by the thinnest hint of a smile which disappeared as soon as it was offered.

"You'll want to be talking to Shayleigh's coworkers, I s'pose. She didn't mix much with anyone, especially me. But they're the ones knew her best. I'm tough on all the girls, you see, trying to keep them safe and all. But Shayleigh sometimes cried after I warned her about some and such."

Corbin paused, his eyes glassing up just a bit before finishing his thought,

"Guess I scared her a bit."

Then, getting worked up again for just a moment he pleaded,

"But they all get careless from time to time, you know? 'Specially near the end of shift ... *They* may get tired, but the spinning machines don't. So, I'm not much for caring about their feelings, if you get my meaning."

At that, his bluster was gone, and sadness again clouded his expression as he led us through the maze of machinery.

As the three of us approached the spinning machines I noticed for the first time just how demanding Jeff Corbin's job was. Time and again, Mr. Colgrove maneuvered back and forth among the three contraptions, pointing out bobbins on the verge of being filled to one ragamuffin, while calling out to another to roll up his sleeve. Then, returning to stand behind a very young woman, clearly new to the task of operating Shayleigh Grogan's spinning machine, Mr. Colgrove finally noticed us. Rolling his eyes in exasperation, he blew out through pursed lips a deeply held breath. His face was red with exertion, the armpits of his shirt soaked with sweat from the sweltering heat, and his suit coat ... well, it must have been someplace, but right now was nowhere in sight. Then, after taking and releasing yet another deep breath, Mr.

Colgrove looked Corbin squarely in the eye and called out over the clattering,

"Glad you're back, Mr. Corbin."

To me, Corbin looked almost too pleased at Mr. Colgrove's condition and effectively dismissed him with a sweep of his good arm, a curt nod ... and nothing more. Mr. Colgrove, at first, appeared completely unfazed by Corbin's attitude, but when he was unable to locate his suit coat, turned to CJ and me with a most disgruntled expression and snapped,

"I'll be in my office if you need anything else."

So there CJ and I were, standing abandoned amid the organized chaos of machinery and people in constant motion. We had no choice but to introduce ourselves to the young women who operated the other two spinning machines. Their names were Charlotte Gilman and Eleanor Monford. They shared severely tied-back hair and the drawn countenances born of exhaustion. Both also appeared so emaciated as to be lost in the grime and stain-covered pinafores they wore over their dresses. However, both were anxious to help.

I was amazed at their ability to operate the spinners, mend broken threads and supervise the child workers, they called doffers, while conversing with CJ and me. So rather than asking pointed questions, we allowed them to simply tell us everything they knew about Shayleigh. While this resulted in lots of information we already knew, enough was gleaned to make our interviews worthwhile.

While Shayleigh arrived here from Ireland only two years ago, Eleanor and Charlotte grew up in the mills. They started as doffers and were promoted to operators in their middle teens. Charlotte was now twenty-one, counting the days until her wedding next April, and made it quite clear that that day would be her last in the mill. Eleanor, on the other hand, was only seventeen, had been an operator for about a year, and couldn't see beyond making it through tomorrow.

Neither of the young women knew Shayleigh very well and given what happened felt badly about it. They felt worse still when they confessed that Shayleigh wasn't very good at her job. In their opinion, it was inexperience with machinery of any sort that was at the root of Shayleigh's problems. While Eleanor and Charlotte could see problems developing, and take preemptive action, Shayleigh always seemed surprised when threads broke, or clogs occurred.

So, she was always here when they arrived in the morning, often worked through her lunch, and stayed late. While Eleanor and Charlotte were always able to count and arrange their filled bobbins for transport to the slashing department during the day's run, Shayleigh often had trouble keeping up and was forced to perform this task while everyone else headed home. They had no idea how late she remained but had overheard Mr. Corbin warn her about remaining after hours; especially this time of year when it's nearly dark by the end of shift.

They'd also heard that Mr. Corbin had expressed to Mr. Colgrove, on more than one occasion, that Shayleigh had no business in charge of a spinning machine. And the facts were, just about everyone on the production floor agreed. But Mr. Colgrove wouldn't listen. Unable to fathom why Mr. Colgrove felt compelled to protect Shayleigh, the rumor mill concocted stories ranging from the innocent to the obscene, which enraged Mr. Corbin and intensified his hatred of Mr. Colgrove. All interesting and enlightening, without doubt.

However, the best bit of information came to light only as an afterthought. CJ and I had thanked the young women and were leaving when Charlotte Gilman casually mentioned,

"It just occurred to me Tommy Peterson hasn't been around since Shayleigh were done in."

That got our attention but good. When CJ pointedly asked who Tommy Peterson was, Charlotte said,

"Why, Tommy Peterson be Shayleigh's favorite little doffer."

Then Eleanor asked,

"Is that important?"

Chapter 20

Where, Oh Where Has the Little Lamb Gone?

It certainly was!

In the short time CJ and I had spent there, it quickly became obvious that to these children the mill was their home, their school, and their playground. They had either parents or other family members working in the mill and were here because of them. So, even when sick the children came to the mill. There was simply no place else for them to go.

However, when CJ and I asked around about Tommy Peterson, we received a combination of shrugs and blank stares. Everyone knew who he was, but nobody could point to an adult responsible for him. From what we could gather, he just showed up one morning with the other children and was absorbed into the mill community. And just as enigmatically, he had disappeared on the same day Shayleigh Grogan was found at the bottom of Witt's ledge.

Coincidence? Maybe. But right now, it was the most encouraging bit of information we had. And so, it was with more questions than answers that CJ and I left the mill.

After we crossed back over Marshall Street and stood on the corner of Center, I stole one last look at *The Adams North Cotton and Woolen Manufacturing Company*. It was then I noticed the behemoth *Harvey Arnold & Co.* textile complex next door and to the north side of the Colgrove mill. The time of its opening and the shelling of Fort Sumter corresponded almost perfectly. And because Mr. Arnold's mill had invested in the most modern of looms available, *Harvey Arnold & Co.* secured contracts to supply vast yardages of fabric required to clothe Union soldiers. Mr. Arnold and his investor brothers, Oliver and John, became very rich, very fast. By the end of the war, the original mill had expanded to several buildings, all of which dwarfed the outclassed and outmoded Colgrove mill.

The "The Print Works" stood prominently, representing progress and the future of North Adams; a juggernaut in the process of crowding out the past. It left me imagining the human toll this affluence exacted from the women, children and men who toiled in mills like these; mills where the owners didn't agonize over every injury and service-connected illness the way Jeremiah's father did. And I wondered how much longer he could hold out. How much longer could he buffer his textile workers from the fate awaiting them just next door?

And so, it was with a mixture of sadness and anger that I wailed to CJ,

"We've got to find that little boy, CJ ... we've simply got to!"

CJ took my hands and looked me squarely in the eye. When he bit his lower lip and inhaled deeply, I knew CJ had several questions, but only asked one:

"Where to?"

I answered CJ's question by looking east, up the corridor of businesses that was Center Street and nodded toward the magnificent gothic chancel looming a quarter mile away, St. Francis of Assisi Church.

"The man best equipped to find lost souls that I can think of is his riv'rence. Let's go talk to Father Lynch, CJ."

As we reached the east end of Center street and crossed Eagle, I couldn't help but marvel at this red-brick cathedral of Catholic worship before me; this dream of Father Lynch made real by the several thousand Irish immigrants who'd chosen North Adams as their adopted home. Situated ten feet above street level and with a steeple nearly two hundred feet in height, St. Francis was easily the tallest and largest house of worship in all of western Massachusetts. Every time I looked up, the gold cross at the spire's apex seemed to be in the clouds.

It was CJ who, as usual, brought me back from that place my wandering mind so often takes me.

"Been to confession lately, Virginia?"

But this time CJ's question served to confuse more than refocus me. When I returned a "What are you talking about?" stare, he continued,

"The center doors of the vestibule are open."

Ah, so that was it. Open doors were Father Lynch's invitation to anyone interested that he was available for confession. However, still only slightly enlightened, I allowed CJ to lead me into the church and we knelt down in a pew next to the confessional. There were only a few people ahead of us, so we didn't have long to wait. And when the last penitent departed, CJ quickly rose and secured the vestibule doors. Finally understanding, I then smiled at him and said,

"Are we really going to do this?"

To which CJ responded,

"Shhhh … we'll never both fit together. Pick a side."

And I did. I entered the right confessional while Conal took the left, and together we sandwiched the unsuspecting Father Lynch in the priest's booth between us.

Once I knelt and closed the curtain behind me, I could hear his riv'rence mumbling prayers. Then, the small privacy door in front of my face suddenly slid back with a clunk. Only a square lace doily maintained my anonymity as Father Lynch's lilting tenor voice greeted me,

"Blessings upon you. Are ya' here seeking God's forgiveness?"

I nipped my tongue to suppress the snicker I so wickedly felt, allowing me to instead curtly respond,

"Not today I'm not. But we do need your help!"

The good father hadn't even gotten my name out of his mouth before I heard a knock drawing his attention to the other side. When Father slammed the other privacy door open, CJ didn't even wait for his greeting, before blurting out,

"Ever heard of a ragamuffin named Tommy Peterson?"

At that, the good father exploded,

"Saints Patrick, Brigid and Colmcille, protect me! 'Tis surrounded by a wailing banshee and her trickster púca, I am!"

CJ and I must have accepted the tongue lashing which then rained down upon us with proper reproof, because once Father Lynch peeked out the door of the priest's booth and saw that no parishioners were left about to observe our mockery of the sacrament of Confession, he pushed our curtains aside, and waggling his finger to come hither, invited us to join him in a pew. Realizing his mock Irish ire had been wasted, Fr. Lynch paused for a few seconds while glancing about to be certain his voice hadn't shattered any of the church's new stained glass. Then he blinked his eyes repeatedly at both of us and whispered,

"What have you two gotten into now?"

At that, I looked to CJ for help. Fully aware of my penchant for hyperbole and emotional outbursts, he gave a quick nod of acknowledgement and proceeded to apprise the good father of what we'd learned, and why finding Tommy Peterson was so important ... all in under five minutes. No sooner had CJ concluded his oration than Father Lynch was on his feet. Removing the purple ribbon stole from around his neck, he placed it, along with his

Roman Ritual, in the priest's booth of the confessional and announced,

> "We'd better get going. We've quite a slog ahead."

Chapter 21

A Reason to Fly

As we set out, Fr. Lynch held true to his personality. He was on a mission and saw little reason to waste either time or energy on chit chat. Instead, he let his feet do his talking. And they had clearly ordered us to keep up if we wanted our answer. The first part of our jaunt took us south and up a knoll to the tree-lined and meticulously landscaped village square where Church Street crossed Main. And because the Methodist, Baptist and Congregational churches occupied three of the four corners, the villagers had aptly named the area, "Church Hill." But the presence of Sandford Blackinton's mansion on the southeast corner of the square also signified that this intersection of Main and Church streets was also the gateway to the most concentrated stretch of extravagant Victorian homes in North Adams.

Alas, when we reached this intersection, the good father made it quite clear that our destination lay in an entirely different direction, both literally and metaphorically. He abruptly stopped and looked east, up the hill of ever-increasing steepness that was upper Main street, and said,

"The Peterson farm, such as it is, is up there."

And with that, the unrelenting force that is the Reverend Charles Lynch left us in his wake to keep pace as best we could. We passed Drury Academy, set back off the street and on the crown of its own knoll to our left, as well as a row of several small homes on our right. However, we hadn't gone on for more than a few minutes before we entered yet another part of the village I'd never visited, or even seen. Main Street abruptly narrowed to little more than a serpentine cart path gouged into the contours of the steep grade looming before us.

CJ and I stopped short, not only to collect ourselves, but also because we were dubious of our destination. We then looked askance, first at each other, and then at Father Lynch because the landscape before us had been completely denuded of trees and was covered solely by scrub bushes and bunch grasses. Hardly what I'd call farm country. Amused, Father laughed out loud; and already on his way called out,

"Well? Are ya' comin'?"

Replete with rocks, ruts and gnarly roots, the going became both slow and arduous. By the time we walked the half-mile required to conquer this rather sheer foothill of the Hoosac Mountains, my two men were sweating profusely; while I, naturally, only glistened.

Standing finally upon level ground, we paused to assess our accomplishment; and turning to look back and down upon the burgeoning village center, caught our breath. It was then, with a final bracing inhalation, that a most offensive odor invaded my nostrils causing me to gag. CJ eyed me with an alarmed glance, but Father Lynch merely rattled his head back and forth, blinked a few times, and said,

"That, my friends, is the signature aroma of the Peterson farm. Trust me, you'll get used to it."

In the distance and to our right, a fenced area of the feculence and muck reined-in two pigs, more chickens than I could easily count ... and a goat. Farther back from the path and sitting upon a hillock above us was a drafty looking plank shack. And behind that, a large field seemingly overrun by a maturing potato crop.

We managed to skirt the animal pen without stepping in anything, and also managed to leave behind the worst of the olfactory insult. As we approached the cabin, we found the front door open, so Father knocked on the door casing to announce our presence. A haggard, shabbily dressed young woman, not much older than I, came blandly to meet us.

"Afternoon, Nell," Father Lynch offered with his best Irish lilt.

Either unwilling or unable to make eye contact with any of us, and seemingly devoid of any affect whatsoever the young woman muttered,

"What 'cha wan' …? I tole you 'afore we ain't goin' church … c'ain't."

"Not to worry, m'am, that's not why we're here," Father soothed.

When he began to explain that we'd come in search of Tommy, Mrs. Peterson curtly interrupted,

"Whatever you think he done; he didn't do it. Tommy's a good boy, 'spectful of ever'body … don' cause no trouble … an' he surely don' steal!"

She then pursed her lips as she jutted her jaw at all of us and continued,

"So, what'cha's wan' him for?"

Father Lynch just smiled, reached out a comforting right hand, and ever so gently touched Nell Peterson's left arm. She started to recoil, but instead reached across and covered Father's hand with hers and the flood gates opened,

"I don' know where he's got to, Father, an' I bin heartsick. Start of summer his daddy tol' 'im he was old enough to do a man's day's work … an' set to beatin' Tommy when he couldn't."

Nell paused to take a breath. Tears began streaming down her face and she nearly whimpered,

"So, one morning when I got up a while back … he was gone. And, God help me, I didn't look."

The conversation had gotten no further when a horse in work harness jingled into view. Driven by a rawboned, dour man of medium height, the poor animal struggled mightily to draw along the ground a package of several tree-length logs, and halted only when the man blew one long, shrill whistle. Unlike his wife, Mr. Peterson, seemed to have no problem showing his emotions. He stormed toward the three of us confrontationally, pointing directly at the good father,

"Whyn't you just git. Don't wan' nothin' to do with you or your church. We've a hard life here and don't got time for such nonsense."

At that, Nell Peterson spoke up with surprising defiance,

"That ain't why they come, Buster."

Angered, Mr. Peterson went from pointing at Father Lynch to positioning himself to level a powerful backhand across his wife's face. If it was possible, Nell both cringed and fled back inside the cabin with such alacrity that Buster had only empty air to hit. It looked to me like this wasn't the first time Buster Peterson had raised a hand to his wife either … or would it be the last. Clearly enraged by his failure to vent his frustration with life upon Nell's face, he turned back to us looking for trouble.

And he got it.

Father Charles Lynch, late of Ballyjamesduff, Ireland, most Catholic agent of God and pastor of St. Francis of Assisi Parish, North Adams, Massachusetts immediately planted a right uppercut to the chin of Buster Peterson, knocking him flat on his back. Nell must have seen the fisticuffs because she returned and was standing in the doorway beaming at the good father. As their eyes met, he growled,

"Don't worry, Nell, we'll find him. We'll keep him safe.

CJ looked at me with rounded eyes and whistled; while I yanked on CJ's upper arm and blurted,

"Yes!"

At that, Father Lynch stormed past us, flexing his right hand, and growled,

"God forgive me, but that felt good! Let's get out'a here."

By the time CJ and I recovered from our shock, his riv'rence had already reached the road and we had no choice but to light out in pursuit. Once we caught up, father punctuated our visit by offering with a mixture of anger and sadness,

"Tommy isn't there. That's sure. I wouldn't be either … would you?"

That was a question requiring no deliberate response, and neither CJ nor I gave one. But it did leave us with a more perplexing one. Then where is he?

Chapter 22
Heeding a Voice of Long Ago

By the time we'd descended back to Church Hill and bid Father Lynch good-bye, shadows had lengthened and colors around us were fading toward gray. Off to the west, the Taconic Mountains were sharply outlined by a golden sky, forewarning the sun's daily retreat behind them was nearly complete. I shuddered when an already chilled breeze seemed to go right through me and reflected that in less than an hour the village would be painted black.

Crossing to the south side of Main, we passed shopkeepers retracting awnings, taking in sidewalk displays, and otherwise shutting down for the day. Frank Beane, the village lamplighter, carried his ladder under one arm and a pail of tools in the other as he pressed to complete his task of illuminating the village center before nightfall. Sounds of revelry, clinking glasses and whiffs of alcoholic vapors escaped the open door of Jamie Doran's saloon and drew my attention as we passed by. I chuckled to myself as I peeked in. No Doc Briggs.

We'd no sooner taken the left onto Bank Street than I could see light coming through the basement windows of an otherwise darkened Village Hall at the crown of the knoll. CJ noticed too.

"Oh, oh. The cell block is lit. Looks like the bar flies have been getting into it early tonight."

I laughed, probably louder than was called for, and added,

"Either that or Francine LeBeau has taken a cast iron skillet to her husband's skull again."

When Conal covered his head with his hands and ran, I chased him as if swinging my trusty skillet … but for only a few steps. Doubled over and grabbing the stitch in my side, I realized we were giddy with fatigue. My stomach also chose that moment to remind me that neither of us had eaten since breakfast, so I begged,

"CJ, can't we wait till morning to tell Da what we've found out?"

CJ stopped only long enough to give me "that look." So, I just sighed, offered a pained smile, and plodded on in his wake.

It was as we rounded the back of Village Hall and reached the stairs leading down to Constable Station's entrance that we heard it. Through the outer door …

through the thick granite walls ... a woman's screeching voice. Opening that door only made things worse. CJ looked at me with the same rounded eyes he'd displayed when Fr. Lynch flattened Buster Peterson. He may have whistled too, but there was no way to know. My ears were already overcome by a voice I thought familiar but couldn't place. And Sergeant Smart's desk was unoccupied, so there was no one to ask. The only way to find out was to open the Captain's office door.

When CJ did, the first thing I beheld was our best friend Jeremiah pacing back and forth along the office's back wall. The distraught look on his face and hunched posture conveyed a side of him I didn't think possible. Jeremiah Colgrove III was overcome with dread. As CJ and I approached him, Jeremiah returned from his remonstrance and strode to usher the three of us back out of the office and closed the door.

"Pater has been arrested for the murder of Shayleigh Grogan ... and Mother somehow thinks screaming at your Da is going to make it go away."

CJ reacted quicker than I, and asked,

"How long ago, Jer? When did you get here?"

"Just a short while ago … the Captain sent a constable to fetch me at the office … wouldn't tell me why, but I knew … it was only a matter of time."

Jeremiah then slumped into Sergeant Smart's desk chair,

"I guess a constable was dispatched to inform Mother as well."

Then, tossing a disgusted glare at the office door, he continued,

'What's sad is, I'm not sure if all *that* is out of concern for Pater or her precious social standing."

I thought for just a second, I saw a tear form in the corner of Jeremiah's eye. But I also knew that any display of sympathy would be unwelcome, so instead, I commanded,

"Get off your arse, Jeremiah. We're going to see your pater."

CJ made it unanimous by practically yanking the chair out from under Jeremiah.

When we opened the cell bock door the three of us found Sergeant Smart sitting in a chair between two occupied cells; one farthest to the left, the other farthest to the right. Both inmates reclined on their bunks. Both covered their eyes with a forearm. Neither reacted when we entered. But Sergeant Smart did. He rose and turned, brandishing an angry demeanor and a swollen right eye.

In spite of the situation and the setting, Elisha's condition struck me as comical. After all, next to the Captain himself, Elisha Smart was the most physically intimidating and capable member of the constabulary. It must have been one very, very tough dosser to get the best of *him*!

When Elisha saw Conal and me, he immediately softened and said,

"Believe it or not, I didn't take the worst of it. Metcalf's arm got broke. Young Cowlin walked into a left and got knocked out cold. If I hadn't had time to draw my night stick that bloody eejit in the right bunk would've taken me down as well. I can't believe he's only got one arm!"

I immediately looked at CJ who smirked knowingly, and shaking his head said,

"Pretty clear to us what *probably* happened, Elisha. Mr. Colgrove and Corbin here nearly had at it when we were at the mill earlier today. What happened this time?"

Massaging his forehead, Elisha winced as he unwittingly brushed his swollen eye,

"As you can imagine, it took a while to get things sorted out. The young boy from the mill who alerted us ran all the way and was out of breath when he arrived. All he could get out was Mr. Colgrove was being attacked. So, we pretty much went in blind. Even after we got the prisoner's one hand shackled to the desk leg … things were still a bit chaotic."

"Poole was sitting in a chair in his office holding a handkerchief up to his bleeding head. Said Corbin took the weapon away from him, ejected the cartridge and threw the gun back at him. Poole was so surprised it cracked him one."

"Cowlin was coming to, but still on the floor shaking the bees out his bonnet. Metcalf was stomping about, clutching his arm close, cursing Corbin and his ancestors.

"Mr. Colgrove was sitting up against a wall gasping for breath because Corbin had nearly throttled him with one arm."

Then Sergeant Smart paused his point by point report for a second and offered just a hint of a smile before continuing:

"The only two people who had their wits about them were Corbin over there and me. He just nodded at the desk he was chained to and told me to have a look. Well, all I saw was a mess of ink stained papers and an overturned bottle of ink. When I looked down at him and shrugged, Corbin called me a name and told me to check the suit jacket pocket. Heck, I never gave a thought to the jacket. It was lying near the desk's edge and seemed to be the only thing neatly placed."

"Anyhow, as I was rustling about, Corbin explained how Colgrove had helped out supervising the spinning machines earlier in the day and was very upset when he couldn't find his jacket as he left. So, when Corbin discovered it under one of the machines at the end of shift, he decided to return it as a peace offering for an argument he said they'd had earlier."

"It was then I came upon what I thought was a carpenter's awl. When I drew it out of the jacket pocket, the handle and blade were covered with dried blood. Corbin saw how shocked I was and nodded toward Mr. Colgrove, calling him a murdering bastard. Then he beamed and said it was too bad we'd arrived when we did because he could have saved the village a trial."

At that, Jeremiah dashed to Corbin's cell, and reaching through the bars to get at him bellowed,

"You're a lying slug, Corbin! *You* planted that pick! It was *you* who raped and murdered that poor girl! You've hated my father since you lost your arm. *He* didn't reach into that machine while it was running, damn it, *you* did! It was your own hubris that cost you your arm! He should have left you to molder in the gutter ... He ..."

Then Jeremiah abruptly ceased his tirade, withdrew his arms from Corbin's cell, and turning back to us, paused. Flushed of face, yet spent of anger, he then strode past us and said,

"Please ... please find the truth ... end this nightmare."

And before either Conal or I could react, he was gone.

And before either Conal or I could say a word, I noticed Mr. Colgrove and Jeff Corbin had both stood up in their cells, their imploring eyes asking the same question Jeremiah had.

And just to add to my distress, Saorla chose this opportunity to check in ...

No pressure, my dearest Virginia, that voice in my head chortled.

You weren't me, you said.
You didn't want to be a Brehon, you said.

You didn't want to be caught between opposing parties.

You just wanted to solve crimes.

Do you finally see they are both the same thing?

Grrrrrrrrrrrrr!!! Shut it, Seanmhàthair!

Chapter 23
A Review of What I Do Know

I don't know if it was frustration or a sense of despondent inadequacy, but I screamed at the top of my lungs and fled the cell block without a word to anyone and didn't stop running till the biting October night slapped me in the face, stopping me in my tracks. My lungs heaved, and as I fought to control both my breath and emotions; my mind cleared, and reason returned.

If CJ and I had learned anything in our visit to *The Adams North Cotton and Woolen Manufacturing Company,* it was that Mr. Colgrove was the good and honorable man I always believed him to be. There was no way he could even have contemplated the rape and murder of Shayliegh Grogan, let alone carried it out. He was blind to a person's station in life. He cared about everyone in his employ. And while it was a fact of life that textile mill work was dangerous, Mr. Colgrove had taken responsibility for the misfortune which had befallen both George the gatekeeper and Jeff Corbin and done his best to make things right.

How many others had he helped over the years that I wasn't aware of?

Based upon the callous treatment workers disabled in other mill accidents had received, combined with the cutthroat nature of the textile business in general, Mr. Colgrove would not have been faulted for walking away from both men. None of his peers would have even noticed. And the workers would have accepted their fate as matter of course. The facts were, Mr. Colgrove's sole expression of ruthlessness extended to out-thinking and out-maneuvering his competitors. Any fear they had of him was of his brilliance and no more.

And as for Jeff Corbin: he may have been a volcano of crude emotions, but he had also revealed a kind and caring heart to CJ and me. He hovered over those in his charge and treated them all with the compassionate firmness of a big brother. So, while his emotional explosion upon learning that Shayleigh's death had, in fact, been murder rather than suicide, it was certainly understandable. And upon further reflection, it seemed obvious to me that by the time Mr. Poole pointed that rifle in his face, Jeff Corbin was ready to be stopped. He'd only tried to shrug CJ and me off and never actually hit anyone.

And despite Corbin's prior suspicions about Mr. Colgrove, it took the discovery of the awl, covered in what he believed was the blood of Shayleigh Grogan, for Corbin to react with such wanton disregard for his own life. When confronted *this* time by Mr. Poole's rifle, Corbin never hesitated. He ripped it away from the secretary, ejected the cartridge and tossed the weapon back. The stunned Poole simply didn't catch it. That's how his forehead got cut.

Even when he'd finally gotten his arm around Pater's throat, something held Jeff Corbin back. He had more than enough time to complete the throttling of Mr. Colgrove before the constables arrived. But despite what he told Sergeant Smart about saving the village a trial, when it came down to it, Jeff Corbin simply could not kill.

That left me with the following truths: Two good men felt responsible for Shayleigh Grogan's death. Both men were in jail. But neither man had killed her. And so, here I stood, paralyzed both physically and intellectually.

No one's aura had conveniently exposed a murderous soul by enveloping me in its black, evil mist as Lemuel Johnson's had in *The Hoosac Tunnel Murders*. I hadn't yet fainted from the malevolent touch of Shayleigh Grogan's murderer either. And *her* spirit had stymied me because she would only reveal certain aspects of her final moments of corporeal existence. For sure, there *was* a murderer out there, maybe hiding in plain sight. I simply hadn't stumbled across him.

Instead, the seven-fifteen from Troy, New York grabbed my attention as it rumbled in the distance, the mournful blare of its whistle announcing the end of a long day's travel and its impending arrival home. I wiped away my tears, looked to the crystal starlit heavens and chuckled to myself that it was a good bet the murderer wasn't on the train either.

But then it began to nag at me …

Just what DID Mr. Colgrove's competitors think? How ruthless might jealousy or fear of him cause them to be? Could any of them be behind this?

At that, I spun around to go back into the constable station and nearly collided with CJ who, on the other hand, was more than ready and had put out both hands to collect me,

"A penny for your thoughts?"

"Conal, we need to talk to Da … Now!"

As we got to the bottom of the stairs CJ and I were surprised when we came face to face with a harried Jeremiah who was in the process of physically ushering his wild-eyed mother out of the station. Although she was no longer screaming, Mrs. Colgrove *did* manage to look down her nose with disdain at the both of us. As she passed, I honestly thought I heard her huff!

I caught CJ's eye as he disgustedly shook his head slowly back and forth. When I whispered,

"How does she do it, CJ? She's barely five feet tall, yet somehow she can make me check if I smell bad …"

CJ, just shrugged and answered,

"It's a true testament to the extent of her snobbery."

Then brightening, CJ winked at me and called out loudly,

"Not to worry, Mrs. Colgrove, Virginia and I will fix everything. We'll save you!"

And under his breath, CJ then asked,

"Do you think Jeremiah will ever forgive me for that crack?"

Together we laughed out loud and walked back into the station certain he already had.

Chapter 24

Where, Oh Where, Has Tommy Peterson Gone?

When we walked into the Captain's office, Da's bottle of "medicinal" Jameson already sat prominently on his desk, surrounded by three empty crystal tumblers standing sentinel duty. Da was standing off to the side, looking out the basement window lost in thought. When I tried to offer commiserations for the harangue he'd endured at the hands of Mrs. Colgrove, Da turned to face us, waved me off dismissively and smirked,

"I shut her out as soon as she opened her mouth. Kinda' sad. Colgrove does all the work. Makes all the money. But she's the one wit' the attitude."

He then poked his finger into his right ear, wiggling it as though relieving pressure and continued,

"Besides, it gave me time t' think."

As CJ and I burst into laughter, Da removed his finger and turning his hand into a halt signal asked,

"So, what do you two think? The evidence says Colgrove did it."

I started to answer, but the Captain again cut me off.

"But I don't buy it, no sir … not even one little bit! Damned convenient, don't ya' think? All the circumstances pointing directly at Colgrove. I probably shoulda' collared 'im days ago too. If it was any other of those chancer mill owners I …"

Da paused to enjoy the vision he'd conjured in his mind, and after allowing that thought to hang on for a moment, continued,

"Funny, how it was only when you two made it clear t' everyone in the mill that the investigation was lookin' elsewhere that Colgrove's misplaced suit jacket magically reappeared wit' a blood covered awl in one of the pockets … right where that hothead Corbin would find it. And the fool took the bait; swallowed the hook, line and sinker, and completed the trap that was set to snare Colgrove. Forced my hand, it did, and I *had* to arrest Colgrove."

The Captain poured a two-finger ration for the three of us, thumped down in his chair and raising his glass to us proclaimed,

"Damned insulting, though, that someone thought I'd believe Colgrove's that stupid!"

Da then downed his drink in one gulp, and while putting down his tumbler with one hand, withdrew an object from his desk drawer with the other and showed it to CJ and me.

"Imagine. The numb-nuts who planted this honestly believed he was puttin' the final nail in Colgrove's coffin. Instead, he may 've just convicted himself. If that *is* indeed Shayleigh's blood on this awl, the person who planted it on Colgrove is directly connected to the murder, at the very least."

Da then took a deep breath and released it. And his countenance went from self-satisfied to tormented.

"I'm sorry, Virginia, but the whole case hinges on knowin'. It may very well prove that the man who planted this is our murderer."

He then waggled the bloody awl at me and asked,

"Was this used t' murder Shayleigh Grogan?"

Suddenly, CJ grabbed the awl out of Da's hand, and stepping around to the back of the desk dropped it in the drawer and banged it shut.

"No! No, it doesn't, Cap. We don't need to put Virginia through this … not yet, anyway. I know you haven't forgotten what happened when Ginger got near Shayleigh Grogan's corpse. And I also know you wouldn't have asked her to touch the awl if you thought there was any other way. But you see, Ginger and I believe there was an eyewitness to the whole thing."

The sense of relief I felt at hearing CJ's words was immediate. Connecting with Shayleigh's spirit had really shaken me. So, I was definitely in no rush to tempt mingling with any of the evil energy which might have been transferred to that terrible instrument.

CJ spent the next fifteen minutes reporting the events of our day and then concluded,

"So, Tommy Peterson has proven himself to be a clever scamp, more than able to survive on his own. We don't know where he's gotten to, but …"

"I know he's alive, Da," I blurted. "I don't know how I know, but I'm certain of it. And wherever he is, I'm sure he's found a haven and is probably hiding close by."

CJ then resumed,

"Yes, I agree with Ginger, Cap. The little bugger worked at the mill for over two months, yet no one questioned his presence. At the end of shift no one knew where he went, or even wondered. He just … evaporated.

Still, he made friends with the other children and Shayleigh favored him above her other doffers. It was as if he could fade in and out at will. So, I'll also bet he's not only safe, but also someplace near."

For a moment that seemed to last forever, the Captain riveted his stare, first at CJ and then me. He then leaned back in his chair until it bumped the office wall and cupping his hands behind his head smirked mirthlessly,

"So, let me get this straight. You're bettin' that this nine-year-old gossoon, this Tommy Peterson, watched, as the only adult in his world who gave a damn about 'im got choked, raped and was given the coup de grace of having a spike driven inta' her brain. He listened t' her screams, watched her futile struggle and never stirred … never cried out … and had the presence of mind t' remain hidden till the killer carried her body away."

Da then returned his chair to its normal position and folding his arms across his chest shot the both of us a less than reassuring look,

"Is that about it?"

CJ then retorted,

"Yes, Cap, it is!"

"And here's why. Tommy Peterson is no stranger to violence … or brutality. The reason he ran away was because his father worked him to exhaustion every day and beat him every night because he couldn't do what a man could. Tommy watched his mother endure daily physical and emotional abuse. And I wouldn't put it past that miserable gobshite Buster Peterson to have raped Tommy's mother while the boy watched either."

"So yes, Cap I'm *sure* Tommy was able to do what you described."

Da again focused daggers at CJ and then at me for that same eternal moment. But then his eyes softened and when he smiled, this time it was with pride.

"You both 've done well. Grand, really. Just grand. We'll follow your lead; but you two better hope the Peterson boy turns up alive, and soon. Because if he doesn't …"

Da stood up and stretched. Then glancing at his pocket watch he concluded,

"In the meantime, I think we should also see what we can come up with to figure out who's behind this. That'll at least give us options. Now let's get outa' here. It's late and there's nothing more t' be done tonight. I'll bet we can bribe Gus t' open the kitchen for us at the Old Black Tavern."

Da then strode out of his office, and as he rushed up the stairs called out to us,

"By the way, I sent word t' Ma earlier in the day that I'd be spending the night in the village. I guess that means I'll bunking in with you two tonight."

Chapter 25

The Best Way to a Man's Heart

The next morning Da, CJ and I were so anxious that barely a word was exchanged as we performed our morning ablutions. Instead we remained withdrawn, lost in our own thoughts. Tommy Peterson was somewhere … but, where? Someone planted that bloody awl on Jeremiah's pater … but, who?

Once on our way to Constable Station, we each strode resolutely, every step a measured increment toward getting on with finding the answers to those questions. The scarcely brightening sky was turning gray-blue, but the air stubbornly held onto its midnight chill, so our breath condensed in puffs before us. The pungent aromas of coal and wood burned in the hearths and furnaces of the village overnight hung heavily around us irritating my nose. The syncopated sounds of early morning village life also echoed around us and made me smile as I compared life in the village to the regimented routine of the O'Leary farm.

Every morning the village resisted being dragged back to life and was revived in the same order the various groups of folks had closed their eyes. The same division of labor that made village life so complex also ensured that it would be close to the noon hour before the process was complete. So different from life on the farm. And I loved it.

Upon our arrival, as we descended the stairs and opened the basement door, we were surprised to find Sergeant Smart already at his desk just outside the captain's office. Rumpled and unshaven, he was filling out the day-shift duty log and drinking coffee. However, other than obviously having slept at the station last night, Elisha appeared none the worse for wear after yesterday's fisticuffs. However, when Da greeted the Sergeant, he looked up, offered only a wan smile and glumly muttered,

"Morning, Cap."

Elisha then nodded at CJ and to me he said,

"Morning, Miss Virginia. Pardon me for not getting up, but ...

Clearly unimpressed by Elisha's travail, the Captain reached across the desk, and gingerly touching Elisha's chin, maneuvered his face from side to side so he could give him the once over.

"Still got the racoon eye, I see, but the swellin's mostly gone down."

Then withdrawing his touch and straightening back up, Da proclaimed,

"By gosh, Sergeant, ya' look fit for duty t' me!"

When Elisha only groaned in response, the Captain chuckled heartily,

"After you get the day-shift assigned, Elisha, get over to see Doc Briggs and have him check you out. And ask him t' come on over to the station when he has a minute. I'd like t' see him. Then I want ya' t' head on home … and for God's sake get some rest! I'll cover for ya' the rest o' the day."

The Captain then turned to CJ and ordered,

"See to Colgrove and Corbin. Get 'em up and get 'em ready for the day. Don't rush 'em, though. Let 'em use the head and wash up. We need to buy some time anyway."

And then smiling at me, Da continued,

"Because you, Virginia, will be using your womanly wiles t' charm Gus into sparkin' up the Tavern's grill early and deliverin' a big breakfast for five. And that'll take at least a half-hour."

When neither CJ nor I moved, but instead offered quizzical looks, Da explained,

"Listen. We need t' find the Peterson boy, right? And we need t' figure out who in the mill had the smarts and the opportunity to set up Colgrove, right? We all agree that neither Colgrove nor Corbin murdered the Grogan girl, right? Well, where better t' start? They're both smart, at the mill every day … and they care. They're involved with more than the process; they know the people. I'm willing t' bet they've soaked up information they don't know they know … And t'is up t' us to draw it out of 'em. That *is* our job isn't it?"

Da's smile then morphed into a cringe as he added,

"Besides, both of 'em had a rough go yesterday, followed by an even rougher night. So, if we hope t' get any help from those two at'all, at'all …"

"Well then, we haven't got all day. Get your arses movin'! In the meantime, I'll get a fresh pot o' coffee on the hock."

As it turned out, more than my womanly wiles were required to stir Gus from his slumber, never mind get our breakfast made. Only banging repeatedly on the Old Black Tavern's door, while at the same time nearly rattling it off its hinges, did the trick.

A bleary eyed, bewhiskered Gus opened the door barely wide enough to stick his head through, and only so he could growl at his tormentor,

"What the hell d' ya' want?"

When I quickly bent forward, planted a kiss on top of his bald dome and followed with the bright greeting,

"Good morning, Gus!"

The transformation was immediate. Gus looked up at my beaming smile and couldn't help himself. His face flushed and his demeanor melted, but the fatigue in his eyes persisted.

"Oh my, Miss Virginia. So sorry. Didn't close till after one last night and cleaned till three. What d' ya' need?"

After I swore Gus to secrecy and explained the Captain's request, he opened the door only wide enough and long enough to slip me in. No sooner had I crossed the threshold than Gus stole a final peek, checked for nosy onlookers, and slammed the door shut. Then reaching down, he snagged his braces and hoisted them onto his shoulders. Satisfied his trousers were secure from dropping around his ankles, Gus solicited,

"Cookie doesn't usually show till around eleven, but if you'll lend a hand ..."

This time, it was I who couldn't help herself. I looped my arm around Gus's and chirped,

"Lead the way, chef Gus. Your apprentice at your service."

Amid the laughs, bumps, and a burned finger or two, our mission was accomplished in short order, but it was still the better part of an hour before Gus and I were wheeling breakfast for five, along with condiments, plates, and silverware toward Constable Station on the tavern's trolley.

As Gus and I carried the trays of food and appurtenances into the Captain's office, I noticed that Da and CJ had assumed their customary positions. CJ was leaning against the outer wall to the left of the Captain's desk, arms crossed and was gazing at his shoes. While Da sat semi-recumbent in his desk chair, boots resting on the desktop, crossed at the ankles. His hands were clasped behind his head and he gazed out the basement window. Both were clearly lost in thought.

When the clattering of Gus's tray being placed on Da's desk rattled neither of the dreamers from their contemplations, I made room for my tray by unceremoniously brushing the Captain's boots away, dropping them to the floor which vaulted his chair upright. When Da gave me his best, "What in the deuce d'ya' think you're doin'?" stare, I looked him squarely in the eye and ordered,

"Pay the man!"

Our mutual stare-down lasted but a few moments, and when it ended in mutual smiles I added,

"And by the way, thanks for the help."

To which Da barked the lame excuse,

"Well ... ya' shoulda' said somethin'."

To which the thoroughly flustered Gus attempted to calm what he believed to be stormy waters by offering,

"Not to worry, Cap'n O'Leary, it's on the house."

To which CJ burst out laughing, paid off Gus in full, along with a hefty additional tip, and said,

"You're a wise man, Gus, not to come between those two. Thank you for your help."

To which Gus sheepishly nodded and escaped this scene of mock dysfunction by closing the door behind him.

To which, the Captain said,

"Bring 'em in right away, CJ ... Time t' see if we can convince our prisoners to become confederates in our plan. And cold food isn't goin' t' do it."

To which, to which, to which ... I sure hope the Captain has a plan, because I have not an idea what he's talking about!

Chapter 26

Played Like a Violin

The next hour was … um … let's just say it was interesting. Da greeted Jeff Corbin and Mr. Colgrove at his office doorway and silently nodded toward his desk. The two grumbling men with grumbling bellies, clearly still angry with each other, entered unsure of what the Captain meant. But Gus's special touch had produced a breakfast of such mouthwatering aroma that the answer became obvious.

They managed to maneuver around where the food was stationed on Da's desk in such a way that they shared but never touched nor exchanged words. Just a pointed finger accompanied by a grunt here, a nod of compliance there.

Not camaraderie, exactly. No, not even close. Just a truce. And the animus they harbored for each other eroded a bit more with each bite they shared of Gus's toothsome breakfast. Eventually an air of civility permeated the room.

Finally, with full stomachs and a second cup of coffee in hand, came the question.

Not from Jeremiah's father. The patrician Pater Colgrove expected and accepted the spread as his due. And it showed. He casually strode about Da's office, sipping his coffee like the lord of the manor, checking out the day's weather through the clerestory windows.

Instead, the question came from Jeff Corbin. Last night wasn't the first he'd ever spent in jail … and the breakfast bothered him. In past incarcerations he'd never been offered so much as a cup of black coffee. So, the ever-mistrustful Jeff Corbin reasoned that this breakfast could hardly have been offered out of the goodness of the Captain's heart. There was always a cost. The only question was what it would be. He wasn't angry about it, just wary. It was simply the way things were … at least for him. So, when he finally spoke up, his deadpan delivery was of a man resigned,

"I'd thank you for the breakfast, Cap'n, but something tells me I'm gonna pay for it. So, what's the fare gonna be?"

Da smiled as he got out of his desk chair, pushed it so it rolled over to Corbin and then parked himself on the edge of his desk.

"Take a load off, Mr. Corbin."

Corbin looked askance: first at Da, then at the smiling CJ who, as usual, was nonchalantly holding up the office wall with his arms crossed. Corbin finally shrugged acceptance and plopped down into the chair, feigning lack of concern as he waited for the answer to his question.

"The cost, Mr. Corbin, will be that ya' stop pounding on Colgrove here. He had nothing at'all t' do with Shayleigh Grogan's death."

"But, the shiv!" Corbin blurted. "It was in his jacket pocket …"

CJ cut him off, matching Corbin's intensity,

"Sure was, Mr. Corbin. Strange though, don't you think? When we were in Mr. Colgrove's office, Ginger invited you to look down at him supervising the girls. He couldn't have been there more than a couple minutes. Did he have his suit jacket on?"

Corbin's expression went blank for just a second. Then his brow furrowed, his lips pursed, and he answered,

"No, no he didn't … So what?"

CJ sauntered over to the Captain's desk, pushed the empty platters to the rear and took up residence on the other corner so that he was now sitting next to Da,

"You were right next to Mr. Colgrove when he turned supervision of the spinning machines back over to you. As I recall, we talked for quite a while in the office before returning to the production floor and you were quite amused at how hard Mr. Colgrove had found your job to be. Soaked with sweat, he was, as I recall."

Not yet quite sure what CJ was going for, Corbin drawled,

"Yeah ... so?"

"Where was the suit jacket, Mr. Corbin? CJ barked.

And following quickly, CJ again called across the room,

"Where'd you put your jacket, Mr. Colgrove?"

Mr. Colgrove's promenade ceased straightway, and his quick interest in the conversation transpiring a dead giveaway he'd been listening all along.

"Why, it was so hot near the machines I took it off, folded it, and placed it out of the way on a spare stool."

CJ was clearly enjoying himself as he nodded his agreement with Mr. Colgrove's response. He then forged on like he was examining a witness in a court proceeding.

"And when you left, Mr. Colgrove? Where was your jacket?"

That did it. Pater smacked his forehead with his palm. Corbin shifted in his chair like he had ants in his pants. Both men knew the suit jacket was nowhere to be found. Mr. Colgrove searched everywhere he could think of before storming off. And even though he feigned lack of concern, I'd seen the satisfaction in Corbin's eyes as he scanned the area for it as well and remember doubting that he would he have told Mr. Colgrove if he did see it. But now that their rage for each other had been lowered to a simmer, both men knew why the jacket had gone missing.

"But at the end of shift, Mr. Corbin, low and behold there was Mr. Colgrove's suit jacket, right where you were sure to find it, complete with the murder weapon in its pocket ... just bulky enough to draw your attention."

CJ paused just long enough to let reality sink in. Then he punctuated his argument,

"And you fell for it, Mr. Corbin! Whoever snatched Mr. Colgrove's jacket knew you, knew your temper ... knew you were spoiling to find proof Mr. Colgrove had killed Shayleigh."

At that, the office became dead silent. Corbin locked eyes with CJ, the grimace of anger and flushed complexion of embarrassment betraying the conflicted emotions he felt. He positioned his good hand on the left arm of the desk chair in preparation of a vaulting attack.

But CJ's relaxed body posture and deadpanned expression caused Corbin to pause for just a second, permitting CJ to punctuate his charge. He whispered,

"So, kill the messenger …is that your answer, Jeff, … to pound on me?"

Suddenly defeated, Corbin slumped back in his chair and exhaled a prolonged sigh.

CJ straightened from his position on the corner of Da's desk, stepped toward Corbin and genuflected before him. Then speaking conversationally, CJ added,

"It's not me you want, Jeff. The man *you* want is back at the mill. You go to work with him every day. You may take breaks with him. He may even call you friend."

"But he murdered one of your young charges in a most cruel and vicious manner. He tossed her off Witt's ledge like so much garbage. Then he planted the seeds of suspicion throughout the work force and waited for the gossip mill to convict Mr. Colgrove in everyone's eyes … including, and especially yours. Then he played your personal foibles like a violin, prodding you into that ridiculous attack which accomplished nothing other than to remove you and Mr. Colgrove from the scene."

"This is a very clever, planful, evil man, Jeff."

The Captain then took over brusquely,

"That alone tells me that the murder of Shayleigh Grogan was not the crime of passion it first appeared to be. It was only a means to an end. And right now, whoever he is has a clear field to his real goal … whatever that is."

"So, I need you t' go back into that mill, figure out who the killer is and report back what he hopes to achieve."

Da then joined CJ in front of Corbin's chair, but remained standing, so Corbin was forced to look up at him,

"But here's the rub. Ya' can't kill him. Ya' can't even rough 'im up. Ya' need t' ferret out the evidence and bring a name to us so he can be brought t' trial. Justice through law, Mr. Corbin. That's my business. That's what I do. That's the way it must be."

The Captain then clapped one of his hands on Corbin's shoulder, and bending at the waist to be eye to eye with Corbin, growled,

"If you do that for me, Jeff, I'll let ya' pull the fookin' lever on the fookin' scaffold's trap door!"

Silence again reclaimed the office walls leaving both Jeff Corbin and me to our ponderances. I can't know his, but I do know mine:

How do they do it? Da and CJ hadn't worked together in almost a year. They didn't plan a thing. They didn't rehearse it. But it happened. It always happened. Amazing.

Chapter 27

Getting down to Business

"I'll do it." was all Jeff Corbin managed to mutter.

"What about me?" Pater Colgrove thundered. The look on his face was priceless, almost that of a child on the verge of being left out of the game.

Da looked down at CJ and together they turned back to Jeremiah's father and grinned mirthlessly. The Captain dropped a hand onto the still hunkered down CJ's shoulder and gave it a squeeze, letting him know that he should be the one to break the news,

"I think you'd better have a seat, Mr. Colgrove."

It was Pater's turn to face CJ, and gleaning not a clue, looked over his shoulder at the Captain. Nothing there either. Not even the hint of a smile remained. In fact, all the stone-faced Captain did was point to the unoccupied visitor's chair and continued,

"Rest assured, Mr. Colgrove, you'll have a part t' play. But I'm not so sure you'll care for it at'all …"

The two men remained locked in stares for a moment that seemed an hour before Mr. Colgrove finally sidled over to the proffered chair and sat down. Only then did the Captain announce:

"You, sir, are still under arrest for murder, or have you forgotten?"

Clearly incensed by Da's proclamation, Mr. Colgrove attempted to rise from his chair, but CJ had seen this act not five minutes earlier by Jeff Corbin. At the ready, he rose first and stepped between Mr. Colgrove and the Captain. CJ then placed his hand on Pater's left shoulder, pursed his lips and raising a brow, tersely shook his head. Mr. Colgrove sank back to his seat and released the deep breath he'd taken in. He then looked back at Da, parted his hands, palms up, and nodded acquiesce.

"Fine, Captain. It seems I don't have much choice. So do tell, what's in store for me?"

"Nothin', Mr. Colgrove … absolutely nothin'," Da answered. "You have no standin' here. So, you'll sit in your cell. You'll eat some food. And you'll trust us. I know it's not exactly a Colgrove characteristic, but ya' need t' recognize that your life is in our hands. And there's not a fookin' thing you can do about it."

Mr. Colgrove crossed his arms and staring across the room at nothing in particular argued with himself for a considerable bit of time. Once he collected himself and rejoined the rest of us, he quietly stuttered through clenched teeth,

"I just wish you all … didn't seem to be … enjoying it so much."

It was then that Da finally risked the smirk I knew he'd hidden of necessity behind his chief constable's mask. He paused only long enough to make sure Mr. Colgrove caught the softening of his countenance before sauntering over to the office window and looking out.

When Conal didn't fill the void, I took matters in-hand,

"Pater, please. Everyone in the village sees you as a brilliant, powerful man; a man who depends on only himself, trusts only himself. You've nurtured that persona and used it in business dealings to the point your competitors bear you grudging respect. However, in at least this case, you've also engendered a hatred so profound that someone has sanctioned the murder of an innocent as a means to destroy you."

Unsure Da wanted me to continue, I paused and looked about. Da was still peering out the office window as if unaware I'd said anything. CJ, who once again leaned against Da's desk, offered me only the quickest of winks and slightest of nods, so I continued,

"What you need to accept, Mr. Colgrove, is that word of your honesty and decency isn't the secret you seem to think it is with the rest of us. It has certainly extended to those outside your family, perhaps further than you're aware. In fact, you can count the Captain among them. He'll never say it, so I say it for him. My Da respects you for who you are and how you've maintained your humanity while surviving in your world."

At that, Mr. Colgrove seemed to implode. His posture rounded; hands clasped together dangled between his legs, his eyes cast down on them. However, far from a man beaten, Mr. Colgrove seemed to finally realize he wasn't alone. Relief replaced acquiescence, and a firm but quiet voice said,

"Thank you."

Da finally turned back to face Mr. Colgrove and sternly replied,

"Don't thank me yet, Mr. Colgrove. What I *think* doesn't count a pile o' horse dung. T'is the *evidence* that does. It tells me what the facts are. You know that as well as I. You also know what we have is quite damning. And my job is t' use it to place a noose around your neck."

Da then exhaled long and slow through puffed cheeks and went on,

"In spite o' that, I've had my doubts you were responsible for what happened t' Miss Grogan, right from the start."

Da must've been amused by what he was going to say next because his countenance again softened for a fleeting moment as he stepped forward toward his desk and winked at me,

"Call it an Irishman's hunch, sir … but the *what* that was done to that poor girl, never fit the *who*. And yesterday's attempt t' force m' hand was transparent, clumsy bollocks. Strange as it might seem, setting you up for the fall secured in my eyes your innocence instead."

Now facing Pater from his perch atop his desk next to CJ, Da's smirk evaporated,

"But it also worked. Every worker on the production floor saw Corbin's outburst when he discovered the awl in your jacket pocket. They also saw both of you taken away in shackles. And they all have mouths, Mr. Colgrove … mouths that I'm sure have been running non-stop ever since. So, it was at that moment my hands became tied. Police work is driven by evidence, Mr. Colgrove, not gut hunches. So here you sit; arrested, incarcerated and soon, you will be charged with the murder of Shayleigh Grogan."

"The only question left is, how soon is soon? How long can I put off Chief Eldridge before he involves District Attorney Ainsley in this? Normally the Chief gives me a free hand. But let's face it. The North Adams Constabulary is only an arm of the Adams Police Department. So, if he chooses, your fate will be in his hands. And once Ainsley schedules your arraignment before a judge, the wheels of justice will proceed quickly and without constraint."

Da darkened further as he continued to lay out the reality of the situation,

"And you, sir, are just the sort o' rich man many folks would like t' see stretched. It'll be a huge political feather in the cap of anyone who gets it done. This case is goin' t' draw statewide attention. And Ainsley, for one, has just the sort o' political ambition that should concern all of us. He doesn't care a hoot in hell about *who* ya' are, Mr. Colgrove, as long as he gets what he wants. In his mind, that feather is his."

"My battle will be t' make sure that doesn't happen."

"Sergeant Mulcahy and Ginger here have their own leads to investigate."

Da then jumped down from his desk, took steps to stand behind Jeff Corbin, and placing both hands on Corbin's shoulders nearly sang:

"And Jeff, here, is goin' t' identify who is goin' t' take your place on the scaffold."

For the first time since I met him these few days ago, Jeff Corbin looked about at all of us, hesitant and in a cold sweat. This hulk of a man who'd spent his life oddly playing the victim, found himself in-league with the very people he saw as responsible for his plight.

This time, "Unbelievable …" was all he managed to mutter.

"Yes, Jeff, I suppose it is," the Captain said. "But regardless o' whatever grudge you may continue t' harbor toward Mr. Colgrove after this is over, know this and know it well. If you fail, Shayleigh Grogan's killer will be free to laugh at all of us till the day we die.

So, there you have it. The Captain is going to protect Mr. Colgrove from a quick trip to the scaffold by confounding the politically ambitious Ainsley. Jeff Corbin is to return to work and snoop around the mill until he figures out who killed Shayleigh Grogan. And CJ and I are to pursue our own leads to find the ever-elusive Tommy Peterson.

Just a scanty few things …

Easy …

However, there was one tiny problem …

We had no leads!

Sometimes, Da's steadfast assuredness drove me to the edge. He gave orders, others carried them out. How? He didn't know any better than anyone else … and he didn't care. The way he saw it, once he dealt them around, they were the recipient's problem. And good luck to ya'.

Then, just to prod his stymied, reluctant charges a bit, Da opened his office door, clapped his hands and smiled,

"Well, get along wit' ya, now. Time's a wasting!"

As the three of us headed toward the door, Da looked Corbin dead in the eye and added:

"Watch your back, Jeff. It's a pooka, you'll be dealin' with … a shapeshifter. He may play the part of co-worker and friend quite convincingly. But this man harbors the worst sort o' evil within his soul. He'll set ya' up, and not hesitate t' kill if he finds out what you're up to. And you'll never see it comin'."

Corbin's only reaction was to sneer and shake his head as he stormed out ahead of the rest of us. He didn't need to say a word. It was clear to everyone that Corbin had just eaten the most expensive breakfast he'd ever had.

Suddenly, the problem CJ and I faced didn't seem so bad.

Chapter 28

Into the Night

Maybe it wasn't. Nevertheless, after nearly a week of in-depth investigation by the illustrious team of O'Leary and Mulcahy, CJ and I were still clueless. Not even a whiff of Tommy Peterson. Nothing.

We'd enlisted every constable in the village to keep an eye out for an unaccompanied, feral-looking boy; possibly dirty, definitely hungry. Their results? Nothing.

We knew Father Lynch would never give up on a lost lamb, whether his parents saw fit to bring him to church or not. So, CJ volunteered to see what the good Father found out, while I was relegated to waiting around the mill's gate at the end of shift in order to reel in as many of Tommy's age-mates as I could. I talked to banders, doffers, and sweepers. If they didn't shave or have hips, I asked them where Tommy was. Some I approached with an, "I know you know where he is, and you'd better tell me," attitude. Nothing.

After two days of this, my frustration built to the point I took the chance of striking up conversations with groups of young women as they headed home to the company row houses: the warpers, the weavers, the spinners and the creelers. They all knew Tommy and liked him, but none of them had seen hide nor hair of him since Shayleigh was done in. Nothing.

All I had accomplished was to wear out some shoe leather and prime the textile mill's rumor pump. When I started, I tried to keep interchanges private. But as time went on, I became careless. Even though I was careful not to reveal why I wanted to find him, they all knew who I was. So, it didn't take a genius to figure out the law was interested in the whereabouts of Shayleigh Grogan's favorite little doffer.

The irony that in trying to save Tommy my damned impetuous nature might get him killed gave me no comfort at all. But it did intensify my desperation to find him. For the life of me, I couldn't understand how a homeless, ten-year old boy had survived for so long without either support or resources. Tommy Peterson seemed to have vaporized so completely I even mulled over the unthinkable … the possibility that he hadn't survived. But no bodies had turned up, juvenile or otherwise. And not one restive spirit had sought me out in the night and interrupted my sleep. Nothing.

To make matters worse, CJ hadn't come home for the past two nights. On the first night, I thought little of it. I assumed CJ had found his riv'rence, and together they were either pursuing a tip someone had given them or discovered evidence of the boy's whereabouts. After all, it's what I'd have done. On the second, however … even though Captain Conal John Mulcahy, captain in the Union Army, and war hero to boot, certainly knew how to protect himself, I found myself nervously peering out our apartment window time and again, positive that *this* time I'd see my beloved walking up Main Street on his way home. But he didn't. So, on that second night, I ate little for supper and slept fitfully in an empty bed. Nothing.

The next morning, the sun streaming in the window helped chase away dreamtime's delusions and loosened the knots in my stomach. Nevertheless, as I set out determined to find my beloved CJ, it was still unsociably early when I cranked the doorbell of the St. Francis Parish rectory. I could think of no place else to go and nothing else to do. However, when the door opened, instead of bringing the good father's beaming countenance to the door, I found myself face to face with a distraught Mrs. Carlson, the rectory housekeeper. When she bawled that Father Lynch was also missing and hadn't slept in his bed these past two nights either, her panic was transferred to me. I bolted without so much as a thank you, and without direction. By the time my stupefaction had subsided, I found myself standing on the corner of Eagle Street and Main … crying.

Chapter 29

Truth in Print?

Get a grip, girl!

Saorla, is that you? Or was it me? It didn't really matter. The thought was a clap of thunder between my ears and served to clear my thinking.

Control what you can, ignore what you can't; and yes, Saorla, indeed, I do need to get a grip.

So, I turned my face toward the morning sun, closed my eyes and drank in the cool autumn air. When I exhaled and turned back to face reality, I found I wasn't alone. There was a world before me, going about its business, living life. But evidently, Saorla wasn't done.

If CJ had left this plane of existence, you'd know, and you don't, so he hasn't.

I was in the process of consoling myself with this thought and placing it back into the corner of my brain where I kept things I knew to be true, when,

"Transcript, Ma'am?"

There before me, little more than waist high, stood a runty lad certainly no older than the boy CJ and I so desperately sought. Looking up at me with coffee colored eyes, his face carried smudges of yesterday's grime, as well as the tired imprecation born of want and need. A parcel of newspapers tucked under his left arm, he raised a single copy of the folded weekly with his right, and nearly placing it in my hand, again petitioned,

"Big doings, Ma'am ... read all about it. What'a ya' say?"

Well, what could I say? I exchanged a five-cent piece for the newspaper. After a cursory examination, the waif gave me a quick thumb's up as he claimed his three-cent prize above the two-cent product he vended and was off. As I watched him go, I called out,

"Do you happen to know a boy named Tommy Peterson?"

His only response was to stop long enough to turn back and shrug. It was then I recalled CJs words: "It's always worst for the children." I doubted this one was able to read one word of the news he spent the day circulating throughout the village and probably never would be able to. I also doubted he tarried even one moment that the cost of the pennies he earned today would be tomorrows doomed to never earn more than that.

When I unfurled the newspaper, there it was. The headline we all feared the most:

The Transcript

Volume LXXII Saturday, October 29, 1866

TEXTILE BARON ARRESTED

by

Wells Mitchell

Rape, Murder and Mayhem Alleged

The village of North Adams remains in a state of shock after learning that pre-eminent citizen and captain of industry Jeremiah Colgrove II has been incarcerated and charged with murder. The arrest warrant filed in Adams District Court by District Attorney Forrest L. Ainsley alleges that sometime on the evening of Friday, October 5, 1866, Mr. Jeremiah Colgrove II raped and murdered one Shayleigh Grogan, a young worker at *The Adams North Cotton and Woolen Manufacturing Company*, owned by

Mr. Colgrove. It is further alleged that Mr. Colgrove attempted to cover his crime by transporting Miss Grogan's body to the top of Witt's Ledge and pushing her over the edge.

When asked for comment, District Attorney Ainsley responded, "I'm quite confident we have the right man. The evidence against Colgrove is clear and excludes any other suspect." Upon a moment's further reflection, District Attorney Ainsley added, "Justice will be served expeditiously. It is my mission to ensure that no one is above the law, not even Jeremiah Colgrove II."

As of this morning, Mr. Colgrove has been transferred to the Adams jail where he will be held until his arraignment at 10 o'clock, on the morning of Thursday, November 1, 1866.

(See: Obituary of Shayleigh Grogan, page 6)

My response was both visceral and immediate. I saw red. That conniving, sleazy excuse for a man Forrest Ainsley had gotten his teeth into Jeremiah's pater. It was well known throughout the county that Ainsley has had his sights set on the governor's office from the first day he took office. For two years now, he's been pining for a case prestigious enough to put him there. And Pater swinging at the end of a rope was just what the doctor ordered.

I'm sure Da had done his best to keep Mr. Colgrove under wraps, but Ainsley had bootlickers everywhere. And I'm sure there was nothing Chief Eldridge nor Da could have said to dissuade Ainsley once word had gotten to him. Furthermore, it was a damned lie to say the evidence excluded all others, and Ainsley knew it. We knew it too. But he didn't care. So, in retrospect, Da had done well to buy even the extra week we'd had to solve this case. But time was up. And I needed to get to Constable Station.

Chapter 30

Truth in Hand

I didn't remember crossing Main Street. And the walk up Bank was only a blur. But this time my incoherence was driven by determination, not panic. I knew where I was going and why. I was simply determined to get there as quickly as possible. When I arrived at the head of the stairs leading to the basement of Village Hall I was seriously out of breath, panting actually. So, I took a few seconds to collect myself before heading down. Arriving like a lunatic would serve no purpose other than to make me part of the problem, not the solution. I'd at least learned that much from CJ.

When I opened the door to Constable Station, I was confronted by an atmosphere even more vault-like than usual. The damp chill in the air quickly transformed my exertion's cooling glaze into shivers, certain evidence no one had bothered to light the coal stove. Not one constable remained for a second cup of coffee before heading out to his beat, probably because there was none to be had. Sergeant Smart was at his desk but didn't even look up from the papers he was attending, let alone offer his usual sunny greeting mixed with the latest village gossip.

The silence was deafening.

So, I quietly skirted the sergeant's desk and walked to the stove. When I opened the grate's door, I found yesterday's coals properly banked, so all I needed to do was add a couple shovels of fuel. By the time I'd set up the coffee pot, the stove was already throwing some heat. And it was time.

"Alright, Elisha, spill it. What's going on?"

Sergeant Smart reluctantly looked up at me as if this was the first he'd realized I was there.

"'Morning, Miss Virginia," he grumbled.

When I crossed my arms, tilted my head, and did my best to give him "that look," the ice cracked.

"Aw Jeez, Miss, where've you been? The Captain's out of control. It's as if all the nit-picky things folks 've done wrong in the past year are being called to account. And if you're unlucky enough to get in his sights ..."

Sergeant Smart pointed the pistol he made of his right index finger and thumb, and using his lips like an instrument, blew me his very best "pop" sound.

"That bastard Ainsley has really set him over the edge. Past couple days, the constables have been making themselves scarce as soon after morning roll call as they can. He keeps calling for Sergeant Mulcahy, but the way I see it, it's you he really needs."

Sergeant Smart then took a deep breath and looking me squarely in the eye concluded,

"It's the first time I've ever seen your Da scared, Ginger."

Sergeant Smart's comment really threw me. I'd never seen the Captain unsure of himself either, let alone on the verge of despair. Reflexively, I found myself looking over my shoulder for my husband.

Damn it, Conal John, where the hell are you? You're his best friend. I'm only his daughter ... his little girl.

So it was with uncertainty I opened Da's office door ... and surprise when I found no one there. I balked at entering and turned to question Sergeant Smart but found him already standing sheepishly behind me.

"Um ... sorry, Miss Ginger, but I had more to tell you. Young Mr. Jeremiah arrived first thing this morning, shortly after the Captain. He was in the office with your dad for only a few minutes. Next thing I know both of them lit out like they was on a mission, you know?"

Sergeant Smart then blew out a long breath, and offering a cringed look continued:

"Only thing your Da said was … well, the question he asked me was quite strange, really. He asked me if the life of a farmer was really so bad."

Hearing that question left me leaning against the door jamb for support. The answer was obvious. It told me *where* Da and Jeremiah were headed. But it didn't tell me *why*. What could Jeremiah have possibly discovered that would convince Da to join him in confronting District Attorney Ainsley in his own office? Both knew full well he was determined to see Mr. Colgrove at the end of a rope, and ruthless enough to squash anyone who got in his way. Whatever it was, m' da was willing to bet his career on it.

I looked up over the sergeant's shoulder at the wall clock above his desk and saw it was nearly ten o'clock and said,

"They must already be there, Elisha. Nothing left to do but wait."

I could only hope the sergeant forgave me for closing the door in his face because there was nothing more to say either.

When I surveyed Da's office the disarray was everywhere. The waste bin was overturned. The visitor's chairs were shoved out of place. A copy of the same *Transcript* I held in my hand was strewn across his desk, a page or two hanging off the edges. Standing prominently atop the tall file cabinet off to the side of the Captain's desk was the bottle of Jameson and its two attending glass soldiers usually kept hidden in the top drawer. That the bottle was out, told me Da truly was rattled. Not a good thing. However, that it was full confirmed two other very good things: Da had not succumbed to the creature's allure, and Doc Briggs had been making himself as scarce as the constables. I love Doc. But if there ever was a time his biting sarcastic nature could send Da 'round the bend, this was it.

I comforted myself with those thoughts as I went about righting the Captain's ship. When that was done there really was nothing left to do but sit at the desk … and wait … and wait … and listen to the wall clock behind me go tock, tock, tock.

Just when I thought I'd go crazy, a perfunctory knock on the office door nearly vaulted me from my chair. When I opened it, there stood Sergeant Smart holding two mugs of steaming, aromatic coffee.

"Thought you might like some company, Miss."

The sight and smell of Elisha's offering set my stomach to grumbling and reminded me that what little I'd had to eat, or drink, was at supper last evening. So, I grabbed, quite impolitely, for one of the cups and took a healthy sip before either thanking Sergeant Smart or inviting him to have a seat. Instead, I responded with closed eyes and a long sigh followed by a nodding expression of satisfaction. The coffee was wonderful and improved my mood considerably. Still, I wasn't feeling particularly chummy. Nonetheless, I offered the sergeant one of the visitor's chairs, while I chose to lean against the edge of the Captain's desk, facing him.

"Thank you, Elisha. You are most kind. In fact, too kind for someone such as me."

Sergeant Smart merely looked up from his cup as he took a sip and smiled.

"Not to worry, Miss Ginger, not to worry."

He paused to think for a second before continuing. And when he did, what he said had us both laughing.

"It seems to come with the job."

That wasn't particularly funny on its face, but it was too true. Both the Captain and I were known to get our Irish up, unpredictably and often, without concern for those who got in the way. No, it certainly wasn't funny, for sure. But that the good sergeant had come to not only expect it, but also accept it, somehow, was. And all I could think to say was,

"Sergeant Smart, you truly are a gem."

We sat together in comfortable silence for a few minutes enjoying our coffee. A silence which also allowed me to revisit much of what had happened over this past month. As I got to the events which brought me here this morning, I recalled something Elisha had said which bothered me. So, I asked him:

"What made you think the Captain needed me more than he needed CJ?"

The sergeant seemed to be caught unaware by the nature of the question because he turned his head askance and bit his lower lip while considering what to say.

"I'm really not sure, Miss Virginia. A feeling, actually. But I've been around the Captain long enough to know when he's barking at the moon and when he's barking to bite, ya' follow? Anyhow, he seemed to be calling for CJ because he wanted company. But when he called for you … well, there was a longing … like you had something he needed."

Well, that didn't help much. But it did pique my interest even more. So, I continued to prod.

"Do you see why this bothers me, Elisha? CJ is not only the Captain's best friend, he's the only person Da trusts to find the flaws in his most difficult decisions. What do I possibly have to offer?"

Holy Saints Patrick, Brigit and Colmcille!

"… Never mind that, Elisha. Tell me: where were you two when the Captain was acting this way? What was he doing?"

My sudden change in demeanor obviously startled the poor sergeant because he stumbled as thoughts spilled from his mouth.

"Um, I guess we were right here, ya' know? I mean, in the office. We was getting ready to go home and I was reporting the log for the day's calls … So he was sitting in his chair, you know, behind his desk … And I was right here, I guess. Well, he's been other-directed something awful lately, Miss Virginia, hardly listening to a word I say. All he does is play with that damned carpenter's awl …"

I didn't need to hear one more word the sergeant uttered. Pressure suddenly built from within causing my ears to ring. Sweat beaded along my brow. The office's chill warded off by the heat I radiated. Without knowing how, I found myself standing behind the Captain's desk snatching drawers open and banging them closed.

And then there it was. In the middle drawer of Da's desk. Still covered with blood, now dried and crystallized. This innocent work implement made evil by the hand of a ruthless murderer.

Or was it? It had been used to set up Jeremiah's pater. So, the blood could have come from a pig ... a chicken ... anything that bled red. The person who did that could even have nicked himself ... It ...

STOP! STOP STALLING!!

The price you'll pay will be small compared to the justice served.

NOW, DO IT!

I started to reach down with my left hand, but for some reason felt compelled to switch to my right as I grasped the awl's handle. There was energy here, all right. A cold, black dankness which began crawling through my fingers and into my hand. The putrid stink of rotting flesh filled my nostrils. Whatever evil that had been transferred to this tool of death sought to overwhelm me ... use me. So, I dropped the awl back into the drawer. And my thoughts screamed out:

STOP!

I've seen your like before. You'll not use me. But you will tell me your secrets.

NOW!

This time when I picked up the awl, I was there. But I wasn't Shayleigh Grogan. She'd already told me what she could. I was he. On that night. Long after the end of shift. And she was there. The girl who couldn't keep up. Working in the shadows of twilight. Pathetic. Unfortunate, I guess. But it had to be done. Too easily. The violence. The rape. The murder. It was all there.

But so was I.

Excited by her terror. Laughing at her pain. Aware of who I was but unwilling to say my name. She'll not know. No one will.

BUT I DO! I know who you are. I AM YOU ...

When I came around I found myself splayed across the desk like a wet dishrag, arms dangling over the edges, shivering in my sweat. The awl on the floor, its secrets revealed ... once again just a tool.

Chapter 31

Siobochain

As I collected myself and straightened up, I found poor Sergeant Smart before me, but backing away. I'd seen that same look of shock and disbelief on the faces of others who'd been unfortunate enough to observe me in action. I don't know how today's vision played out before the sergeant, but if what people had told me of my past performances was any indicator of my display … Nevertheless, I didn't have time for explanations or concern. So, I tersely said,

"Tell the Captain I know who the murderer is, and I've gone to confront him."

I was out the office door and half-way up the steps by the time Sergeant Smart reacted and caught up to me.

"Miss, wait. You can't go off on your own."

When I didn't stop, sergeant Smart reached out and grabbing my arm, pleaded,

"Ginger, please. I can't leave the station unattended, even for this. Can't you at least wait till the Captain returns?"

I turned, and looking the six-foot constable sergeant straight in the eye, growled,

"Look, Elisha. I've touched this man's soul. He's terrorized, raped, and murdered ... and discovered he likes it. He's also turned events on their head so Mr. Colgrove will pay for his deeds."

I don't know if it was what I said or the look in my eye, but the sergeant acquiesced. At a loss for words, he released my arm and stepped back. Both of us knew full well that this mountain of a man could stop me if he so chose. But both of us also knew he wouldn't.

As I resumed hurdling up the remaining stairs I offered Elisha one final reassurance he was doing the right thing,

"And he's planning to do it again. Right Now!"

I don't know how I knew this, or what made me say it, but of this I was sure: our spy had been discovered ... that meant Jeff Corbin's time was running out. And it was my fault. I could have stopped all of this a week ago by simply picking up the awl when Da wanted me to. But because I was afraid of what I might have seen, or where a vision might have taken me, I gladly accepted the out CJ provided me.

There, I said it. I was afraid! And because of that, Jeff Corbin might die.

It took only a few minutes to make tracks down Summer Street; follow State until I reached the corner of Main, and then cross to the west side of Marshall. By the time I'd arrived at *The Adams North Cotton and Woolen Manufacturing Company*, George had already opened the gates to greet me, but found the friendly conversation he expected to have reduced to a wave as I sprinted by him and through the entryway. As he tentatively waved back, I could only think that all the shoe leather I'd worn out loitering about these gates this past week finally paid off.

On the verge of closing the last of the hundred feet leading to the mill's front door, I thought I heard my name called out … or did I? I hardly broke stride because the way things were going, the distant voice I may have heard could have been the wind. I shook my head and decided to ignore the sound and reached for the door handle. Then the voice calling my name became two. Two voices I now recognized: Father Lynch! CJ!

My progress suddenly arrested, I turned to find CJ and the good father still quite a way off, walking along Marshall, still outside the iron-slatted fence. Although my sense of relief at seeing them both safe was heartfelt, I also knew there was no time to waste. So, I barked,

"It's Poole!"

When I reached back for the door handle yet a second time, I found myself halted a second time by CJ's voice.

"I know!" followed right after by Father Lynch's. "Yes, *we* know!"

More than a bit intrigued, I turned, yet again, to see my two prodigal men still standing on the other side of the fence. But this time I also noticed the diminutive figure between them. Tommy Peterson! They found Tommy! My elation could not have been higher. Now, we really had that gobshite Poole! However, a thought now rebounded painfully between my ears.

"Get on with it!"

"NOW!"

So, I opened the door, and as I entered I heard what could only have been a gunshot. My elation was instantly replaced by despair. I was too late. But maybe not. Maybe he missed. I ran through the opening room and past shocked workers, up the short set of stairs which led into the mill room. I found myself at the base of yet another set of stairs, these leading to Mr. Colgrove's office. I looked up. And there he was. Poole. On the landing just outside the office loft he shared with Mr. Colgrove. Holding that damned carbine. The puff of smoke from its firing still enshrouding him. The stench of burnt gunpowder stinging my nostrils. And the body of a one-armed man laying at his feet.

Fury overcame me as I stomped up stair after stair. Poole looked down, and immediately putting on the face of innocence and surprise, acted as if he couldn't believe what he'd done.

"It's that maniac Corbin. He was coming at me. Said he was going to kill me. I had no choice …"

Undaunted, I kept climbing and screamed,

"Bollocks! You set Corbin up to attack you, just now, like you did when he went after Mister Colgrove. You knew he couldn't resist. And when the Captain saw through your plan to get Colgrove arrested, you planted that awl. You're a murdering son of a bitch, Poole, and you don't care who you hurt."

Hearing this, Poole's demeanor immediately changed. His pained, benign countenance morphed into one sneering with rage. He quickly ejected the rifle's spent cartridge and smoothly reloaded with one he took from the watchpocket of his vest. Then, as he calmly cocked the carbine and brought the sights to bear on the center of my chest, he hissed,

"No, I guess I don't."

The delivery of those words froze me where I stood, and I prepared to die. Strangely, my focus followed the length of the rifle's barrel, a scant few feet from me, until my eyes locked with Poole's ... And then it happened. I didn't plan it. It had never happened before. But I saw myself as if looking through Poole's eyes. And he must have seen himself through mine because he hesitated. He didn't fire. Something kept telling me I couldn't shoot myself ...

It was then I heard heavy footfalls pounding the lower stairs and a tiny voice screech from the floor beneath them.

"There he is. Him that done it ... Poole! ... MURDERER!"

Poole's eyes broke contact with mine and I was once again me. I watched him look beyond me, searching to locate the voice's source. And once he'd found it, the hatred in his eyes was replaced by bewilderment. When I too looked down the stairs and beyond my climbing savior, I saw what Poole must have seen. Pointing up, directly at Poole, was Shayleigh Grogan. Alive, whole, and yet … ethereal!

I turned back to face Poole and saw that he'd lowered the carbine's barrel; the terror and confusion written on his face a dead giveaway of his uncertainty whether to fight or flee. I used the moment to steal another peek; but this time the voice at the bottom of the stairs belonged not to Shayleigh Grogan but to Tommy Peterson.

I had no idea how long Shayleigh's shade would mask Tommy from Poole's consciousness. But as I turned back, I beheld Poole's look quickly change back from muddlement to desperate rage. It was then I became certain that Poole's next act would be to fire the bullet in that carbine at whoever he saw through its sights; Shayleigh or Tommy, it didn't matter. He wanted them both dead.

It was in that flash of a moment my own fear vaporized. I could not allow yet another innocent to die. So, I closed the distance between Poole and me, and blurted out the first thought that came into my head.

"You'll burn in hell this day, Mister Poole."

Startled, Poole refocused his look of murderous hatred back to me. As he did, he tried to bring the rifle back up but found my left hand blocking its barrel. So, he quickly stepped back once, then twice, to gain the space he needed. On the second step, Poole caught his heel on the prostrate body of Jeff Corbin, causing him to lose his balance and stumble backwards. Now out of control, Poole fired wildly as he broke through the landing's railing and was gone over the edge.

Suddenly, it was over.

It took only seconds for CJ to reach the landing where I stood, still wild eyed, my lungs heaving. I appreciated his attempted embrace but rejected it, nonetheless, even as it was offered.

"Corbin, CJ!" I cried. "Check him. He's got to be alive … He's gotta' be."

Please, Lord, Let him be alive. Please!

But he wasn't.

When CJ rolled Corbin over, his shirt front was soaked, and there was an additional pond of blood on the floor where he fell.

"Dead center, Virginia. The minie-ball must have shredded his heart. It's the only way a man can lose this much blood, this fast. I'm sorry … he's gone."

I hardly knew Jeff Corbin. And what I did know could be said of any man. He was good ... and bad. But he cared ... about justice, about people, about Shayleigh Grogan.

I found myself on my knees beside Corbin. Pounding the floor and wailing as tears streamed down my face. It was then I understood, in some small way, what I thought I never would: the abject anguish CJ felt that day nearly a year ago in the bloody pit.

We'd caught the man who sponsored the murder of Ned Brinkman, Billy Nash, and Ringo Kelly. And even though he laid before us, dying a most horrible death, CJ tried to bash his skull in with a boulder.

It turned out that fate had delivered this man, Charles A. Cousins, who above all others was the root of the demons which haunted CJ. It was the then General Charles A. Cousins' indifferent and callous leadership of Union forces on that spring morning at the Mary Dunn Farm in Virginia that cost the lives of CJ's men. Yet, somehow, CJ felt responsible. If only he'd just ... they'd still ...

It was the Captain's words that brought him to the epiphany. I'll never forget the exchange:

"CJ ... Conal, me boy ..."

"… Let it go, Conal … Let it go. 'Tis time t' heal … 'Tis time t' bury our dead and trust in God's justice."

It wasn't perfect but as it was enough. CJ could finally accept that the loss of his men was not his fault. Indeed, it *was* time to heal.

This time it was CJ who knelt beside me, hugged me in the sweetest, most comforting way. And when he whispered in my ear,

"Ginger, it's not your fault."

I was at peace.

Chapter 32
Let the Healing Begin

My *soul* may have been at peace, but my heart remained heavy, my mind restless. Night after night, my dreams played out the same series of events, ending with Corbin lying at my feet, his life essence spilled over the floor.

I saw Poole roughly grab aside a young doffer, and showing the boy a shiny coin, say,

"Want to earn another coin? Find Corbin and tell him you heard he wanted to know who nicked Mr. Colgrove's jacket. Let him know I gave you a coin to do it and you thought it was just supposed to be a joke. But when Mr. Colgrove was arrested, you got scared and told no one till now. Can you do that?"

When the boy tried to snatch the coin from Poole's hand, he knew he had him. Grabbing the coin back, Poole mirthlessly smiled down at the boy and said,

"After."

Then I was in the Captain's office, again watching Da warn Corbin:

"Watch your back, Jeff. It's a pooka, you'll be dealin' with ... a shapeshifter. He may play the part of a co-worker and friend quite convincingly. But this man harbors the worst sort o' evil within his soul. He'll set ya' up, and not hesitate t' kill if he finds out what you're up to. And you'll never see it comin'."

I also saw Jeff's dismissive response.

But in my dreams, I didn't remain silent as I had that day. I didn't hide behind CJ's words. I called out to Corbin, louder and louder each succeeding night,

"Jeff, listen! Please!"

In the end, it made no difference, even in my dreams. Nuance was not part of Jeff Corbin's makeup; knee-jerk belligerence when provoked was. So, when Jeff swallowed the bait yet again, Poole was ready.

Indeed, it *was* almost too easy, or so Poole thought ... until I climbed those stairs, and Tommy Peterson's words hit him between the eyes.

And so, a week later, I sat at the Colgrove banquet table, exhausted, my head full of cobwebs, surrounded by family and friends as they celebrated the same events which continued to trouble me so. Who *was* Rufus Poole, anyhow? And why had he done what he did?

I wished I was like the others who were so saturated with relief there wasn't room in their minds to consider anything else but congratulations.

Tommy Peterson had been found alive and safe living with the Pyms in Notchboro. After he fled the scene of Shayleigh's murder, Tommy did his best to become invisible. At night, he snuck into the cellars of homes by sliding down coal chutes and sleeping next to the furnaces. By day, he trolled the back doors of inns and scrounged through trash cans for food.

That's where Freddie Pym found him early one morning on his next trip to the village after the murder. Gentle man that he is, Freddie hid the boy under a tarp in the back of his wagon and brought Tommy home like a lost puppy. And there he stayed until Father Lynch and CJ, who'd talked to enough people with broken-latched cellar windows, and inn keepers who'd chased the boy away, to finally figure out where Tommy had gone.

Shayleigh Grogan's murderer was burning in hell. Pater Colgrove had been released and delivered back to

North Adams as soon as the Captain's telegram reached Chief Eldridge.

Wells Mitchell, bless the sweet man, published a full page article in the Transcript which both exonerated Mr. Colgrove and forced District Attorney Forrest L. Ainsley to declare his own mea culpa, for all of Northern Berkshire to read. While the pompous Ainsley may have tried to disguise his naked ambition as a quest for justice, Mr. Mitchell would have none of it. Because he'd also interviewed Da and Jeremiah, CJ and me, he knew the truth and was able to lay out in apple pie order the evidence which not only cast serious doubt upon Pater's guilt, but also pointed out that Ainsley had known about it all along, leaving only one possible conclusion: Ainsley's arrest of Mr. Colgrove was a cruel rush to judgement.

However, Wells saved his final stroke for the Transcript editorial on page two, titled, *Forrest L. Ainsley esq., Servant of the People?* Its focus was clear. Ainsley's actions were not only rash and ill-conceived, he'd also attempted to use the newspaper to convict Pater before the trial was even held. And all of it solely to advance his own political ambitions.

It wasn't perfect, but it was the best Pater could have hoped for. Ainsley would hold his job for now. But come next election, folks would have much to consider.

The impromptu hit of the evening came, however, as dessert was being served and Da impersonated Ainsley's puffed-up, officious attempt to save face with Wells Mitchell:

"Bwuh-huh-hum ... But of course, Wells my man, you realize that the arrest of Colgrove, here ... and everything I said about him ... was just a ruse."

(pause, as Da looks at the ceiling and taps his chin with his forefinger)

"Yes, yes, that's what it was. All part of *our* plan to draw the real murderer out. Right Captain O'Leary?"

(silence)

"Right, Sergeant Mulcahy?"

(silence)

"Right, Jeremiah, my boy?"

(Together, Da and CJ make the chirping sound of crickets, raise their glasses in toast to Pater, and take a drink)

(the dining room at the Colgrove mansion reverberates with laughter)

Even the slightly inebriated Mrs. Colgrove must have seen the levity in the Captain's delivery because I caught her out of the corner of my eye raising her napkin to cover the wine which had escaped her up-curled lips and dribbled down her chin.

Ma elbowed me and nodded in Mrs. Colgrove's direction; but the quick wink I returned let her know that Mrs. Colgrove's faux pas had been duly noted.

Then Ma leaned over and whispered in my ear,

"Speakin' o' droolin' tipplers, where's Doc?"

Scanning the room I smiled at Jeremiah, Father Lynch, Da, and CJ; and I was indeed surprised to find one empty chair. Where *had* Doc gotten off to?

The Captain must have heard Ma's question because he whispered,

"He stopped by the constable station this mornin', bright and early. Said he was takin' the train t' Springfield. Wouldn't tell me any more than that. Guess he hasn't gotten back."

The tinkling of silver against crystal ended our private conversation and drew all eyes to Mr. Colgrove who was standing with a glass of wine in his hand. Nodding to all, he began,

"I don't know how many times I've thanked you all for rescuing my chestnuts from the fire, but tonight I'd also like to thank you for what you've taught me about trust and friendship. Both are so hard to come by in this world, it's easy to forget they exist."

With that, Pater raised his glass and said,

"Captain O'Leary, Sergeant Mulcahy, Father Lynch, and of course, Virginia. Thank you on behalf of Shayleigh Grogan. You've worked yourselves to exhaustion. You've risked your lives. You've looked death in the eye, ... all to avenge the evil done to this young girl. I'm sure we'll always keep a place in our hearts for Shayleigh Grogan. May her soul rest in peace."

At that, Pater invited us to join him in the toast. He then put his glass down on the table and sat down.

Jeremiah then exchanged positions with his father, assuming the floor,

"During this past week, Pater and I have had quite a bit of time to talk and do some soul searching. Indeed, truer words were never spoken when he mentioned how hard trust and friendship are to come by. Once you find them, you dare not throw them away. So, I'm here to set things right."

"CJ, from the first day we met I've considered you a friend. Over the past year you've become my brother, my guide to finding my better self. I trust the judgement of no man more than I do yours."

"Ginger ... have we ever *not* been friends? Teachers didn't like us. Students didn't like us. The best I can remember, there were times we didn't like each other. But I'd like to think that our friendship became more than a hedge against aloneness. There always has been a kind of love which persists to this day ... a love we have trouble explaining to others. No one can put me in my place like you. You keep me humble."

When the room burst out in laughs and guffaws, Jeremiah flushed; and pushing air toward everyone with outstretched palms, he too chuckled,

"How about less arrogant? Does that work?"

"Bottom line, I need you both in my life. But so does the Captain."

"So, here's my proposal: The law firm will reorganize. I will continue to handle the corporate work and hire an associate to deal with the overflow. CJ, you will oversee the quality, ethics and integrity of all corporate work. No deal will happen without your approval."

"Ginger, for this to work, the firm will need to employ an investigator. Someone who can establish the veracity and integrity of the people on the other side. You will protect our clients and the firm from all malintent. No deal will happen if you recommend against it."

"What I'm saying is, I want ... no, I need you both ... as full partners. And the law firm's new name will be *Colgrove, Mulcahy and O'Leary: Solicitors and Investigations.*"

"And Captain. I haven't forgotten you. In spite of recent events I don't see the Adams Police Department ever adding a detective branch to the constabulary of the north village. Do you?"

"So, I propose that Conal and Virginia spend one day per week as consultants to the North Adams Constabulary. Furthermore, should events dictate, their services to the constabulary will remain the priority of this firm as long as needed."

At that, Jeremiah shook his head and grinned,

"Actually, I don't see how I could stop them."

CJ then held out his arms in supplication and asked,

"Well ... what do you all think?"

Mrs. Colgrove surely let everyone present know what she thought when she pushed herself away from the table in a huff and left the room. When the two Colgrove men ignored her, they made clear what they were thinking as well.

Just then, the front door of the Colgrove mansion banged off the wall and a voice echoed throughout the vestibule,

"Been a long day. Anyone in there care to offer a man a drink?"

Doc!

Chapter 33
Rufus Poole

When Doc Briggs entered the dining room and unceremoniously plunked his tired bulk down at the table, he carried with him the distinctive suggestion of a man who'd spent the day elsewhere and travelled hard upon his return. Soon, the moist, earthy aroma of outdoors, laced with the fumes of burned coal, filled the room for all to *enjoy.*

A huge grin spread across his face as Doc leaned back to complete his much-practiced routine of firing up the disgusting cheroot he'd pulled out of his suit jacket pocket. A match seemed to appear from nowhere. The three, quick, room-fouling puffs Doc inhaled also had the predictable result of triggering tearful coughs so violent he dislodged the ash, and the damned stogie went out.

Once recovered, Doc clamped the now extinguished stogie between his teeth, and surveying his table mates found all eyes riveted upon him. He now owned the room, just as he intended. And also, not surprisingly, he was going to milk it.

"Well? Where's my drink?"

When the Colgrove's butler placed a stemmed glass of wine in front of Doc, he looked up and said,

"You're kidding, right? Come on, Neville, bring me a proper man's drink."

Neville, who knew Doc well, was far from insulted by the response. Instead, a hint of a smile accompanied the quick nod he directed toward the table maid, who'd already fetched a tray carrying a single crystal tumbler and a decanter of the requested amber liquid.

"Ahhh, that's more like it. Thank you, Jenny."

Doc then waved off Neville's attempt to pour and said,

"After today's events I'll require a bit more of this tranquilizer, here, than you usually dole out, Mr. Matt."

Doc then raised his glass to admire it, and with the words, "Doctor's orders," downed its contents.

When he reached for the bottle to refill his glass, Pater beat him to it, snatching it away.

"Enough, already, Doc! Not another drop of my personal stash will cross your lips until the truth of where you've been this day does. It must be good, or you wouldn't be having us on like this. So, spill it, damnit!"

Unblinking, Doc merely laughed and parried,

"Telling my story's going to be thirsty work, Jer … damned thirsty work."

He then held out his glass to Pater and giving it a swirl tilted his head toward the decanter. Pater let out a sigh and filled Doc's glass. The rest of us exchanged knowing glances. After all, we'd all played this game before as well.

Remarkably, Doc took only a short sip and put down his nearly full glass before commencing.

"Been bothering me as much as you about who this Rufus Poole character was. Single blokes like him are usually drinkers or gamblers or womanizers. You know, men after my own heart."

Doc then gave a chuckle, took another sip and said,

"Indeed, I take great pride in knowing those who may provide me a hedge against boredom. But Poole? Nothing. Never even heard of the man. And I couldn't reconcile his actions with the life of a saint. So, I stopped by to see the only bloke in the village who lives closer to the gutter than I do … Dutchy Gregory. All he could tell me was Poole came from Springfield. Which brings us to today, my train ride, and what I was able to dig up."

"I was convinced a crumb like Poole had to be wearing some very filthy underwear. So, my first stop was to see a chap I used to run with in my days at Amherst. Works in the Hampden County District Attorney's office. If Poole had so much as spit on a sidewalk in the past twenty years, he'd not only remember when, he'd know the name of the street. Cost me a bottle and lunch, but here's what I got."

At that, Doc made a great production of reaching inside his suit coat pocket for a single, length-wise folded sheet of paper which he flattened on the table, and then promptly ignored.

"Rufus Abner Poole. Born 1840. Parents, Franklin and Martha Poole. Both parents were in service to Colonel Harold Stoughton, superintendent of the Springfield Armory. Father was estate caretaker, mother a downstairs maid. As a young boy, Poole was expected to be companion to the family's son. That meant doing whatever the son wanted to do whenever he wanted to do it. So, he was more servant than companion."

"At age ten the Stoughton boy was off to boarding school. Poole was left to work with his father. That meant he helped care for the grounds in the summer and shoveled coal to keep the grates filled in the winter."

"His mother saw to his studies. But lessons were intermittent and only after the workday was finished. So, they were always by candlelight and when everyone was exhausted. Nevertheless, Poole was driven to learn. And once his mom taught him a lesson, he practiced on his own till he mastered it."

"Early on, Poole figured that if he was to rise above his station, he'd need to be smarter, and that meant better educated. So in addition to studying and practicing to exhaustion, he paid sharp attention to the patriarch; how he dressed, spoke, and interacted with other people."

"By the time Poole was in his early teens, he'd learned his part well and used his time with Master Stoughton to test himself and to curry favor. The Stoughton boy responded by treating Poole as a friend. He even shared his clothes with Master Poole so he could bring him along while attending social activities of the Springfield elite … which, interestingly, included hunting trips. Incidentally, I understand Master Poole became quite adept around firearms."

Doc paused a moment to let that sink in and raising and eyebrow, took yet another short sip,

"Over time, the more Poole experienced the gentleman's lifestyle, the more he resented the life he returned to at the end of each day. He began ditching his estate chores and even took to looking down his nose at his parents. When Rufus was seventeen, he and his father came to blows over these issues. This brought the entire Poole family before the patriarch's justice. The Colonel informed them that either the boy left or the whole family would be sacked without references."

"So, late that night, while everyone slept, Rufus Poole decided he'd had enough. But before he left he paid a visit to young Master Stoughton, who gladly supplied his friend with a suit of clothes, shirt and tie; a pair of shoes, and an overcoat. Thus outfitted, Poole departed, and his ten year charade began."

"By the time he'd applied to become your secretary, Jer, he'd been a veteran of several scrapes with the Springfield courts. Rufus A. Poole, salesman. R. A. Poole, Esq. Attorney at Law. Abner Poole, Real Estate Sales. You name it. If there was a possible source of loose money, he tried it. And each time, he stole, embezzled, or proved to be a fraud."

"But his incarcerations were short ... and with every failure, he got a little better at the game. What remained hidden from all of us was a heart which had also grown darker and darker. He'd become capable of doing anything to serve his own needs."

"As near as I can figure, all of this was to take over your mill, Jer … to move you out of the way. Knowing young Jeremiah's interests lay elsewhere, he'd be named manager … and become a textile mill aristocrat."

After downing the remaining contents of his tumbler, Doc enjoyed the stunned silence pervading the room, before asking,

"What's a man need to do to get a proper drink around here, anyhow?"

At that, Doc held out his glass which Pater Jeremiah Colgrove promptly filled to the brim.

Chapter 34
Perfect Solutions

The next morning, as the partners of *Colgrove, Mulcahy and O'Leary Solicitors and Investigations* met for their inaugural meeting in the firm's library, it wasn't clear if we'd all fully recovered from Doc Briggs' pronouncements. Jeremiah walked in quite kempt and impeccably dressed. However, both of us knew that was no barometer of how he'd slept. But I do know that *our* rumpled appearance was. CJ and I spent much of the night bouncing each other about the bed until we finally got up and resolved our perturbations over hastily brewed cups of coffee.

Although it was a fact that jealousy and animus toward the Colgroves for their financial success caused some competitors to seethe, it was also a fact that the *Adams North Village Cotton and Woolen Manufacturing Company* was dated and inefficient compared to the monstrosities popping up along the banks of the Hoosic River. Its name was larger than its profits, and hardly a threat to anyone. Moreover, it represented only a tiny fraction of the family's holdings. Logging, the sawmills, the grist mill, expanding real estate holdings, and now the law firm made up much bigger portions.

So, there was no conspiracy perpetrated by rival mill owners; just the actions of a small-minded, evil man who was willing to rape and bear calumny against a man with a good heart.

It was CJ who brought me back from my ruminations, as usual.

"How's Pater doing this morning, Jeremiah?" I asked.

"I'm not sure, actually. He was up and gone by the time I rose. Neither Neville nor Cook had an answer …"

Jeremiah then grimaced for a second before continuing,

"And I doubt very much that Mother did either. Actually, there was a definite chill in the room during breakfast."

Jeremiah's next pause was also a short one. What he said nearly burst from him and knocked us from our chairs.

"I've given Mr. Matt instructions to have my belongings delivered here and brought up to the third floor apartment … Looks like I'm going to be your neighbor."

CJ and I looked at each other in complete shock. It was CJ who asked,

"Does Mr. Colgrove know?"

"Oh, yes. It was the last thing we spoke of before retiring last evening. As I recall, his only comment was to ask if he could join me."

If Jeremiah's answer hadn't been so damned calamitous, it would have been funny. But no one laughed. No one even cracked a smile. Only CJ responded,

"Have you told her, Jer?"

"Who? Mother? Why? She hasn't paid a mind to anything I've said since I returned from law school. Anyhow, I think my intentions will become obvious when Neville and Miles start loading my belongings onto the buckboard."

When both CJ and I glared looks of disapproval at him, Jeremiah blinked before we did.

"Yes, yes. At least I've learned *something* from you two over this past year. I know what I need to do … But I guess I sometimes still lack the resolve to follow through."

It was at that time the back door of the building opened, and what sounded like a herd of horses came into the entryway. Along with the rustling of coats being shed, and the clomping of booted feet, intermittent voices colored the tumult approaching us down the corridor.

First to enter the law library were Pater and the Captain, still rubbing their hands together against the November chill they'd just escaped. They grabbed seats at the conference table and nodded their greetings. Father Lynch was next to come through the doorway, holding hands with two bedraggled, obviously intimidated people. Tommy Peterson … and his mother Nell!

I immediately got up and taking Tommy's other hand gently offered him a chair. Father Lynch gave Nell a final pat on the back as he pointed out a seat for her before assuming his own. Once we were all gathered, we took turns looking about the table at each other. But no one spoke. No one knew quite what to say. Even if you knew why *you* were there, you hadn't a clue why the others were. The puzzlement didn't last long, however, when the Captain spoke up in his most captainly manner.

"Just got back from the Peterson place."

"A boy needs his ma."

"Tommy was without his."

"So, we went and got her."

Da's face then lit up as he recalled the memory,

"The good father and I made Buster Peterson an offer he couldn't refuse."

When Jeremiah, CJ, and I shifted our attention toward Father Lynch, he only responded with upturned palms, a shrug, and a smile. So, Da continued,

"Yes. Buster must've noticed us approachin' that shack they live in because he came stormin' down from his upper field as soon as we crossed his property line. Now, a smart man would've seen the two of us knockin' on his cabin door and been a bit careful. But not Buster. Screamin' his head off, he was, actin' in a most threatenin' manner. Well, what could I do, bein' a peace officer and all?"

On cue, CJ then chortled and broke in,

"You knocked him on his keester?"

"Only in such manner as was necessary to stabilize the situation, Sergeant … And I did help him up and dusted 'im off once his eyes were able to focus again."

The giggles near the end of the table belonged to Nell who was obviously feeling more and more relaxed as she listened to the retelling of the morning's events. Her voice was as strong as I remembered when she added,

"Father Lynch then come inside 'n' tol' me what happened t' Tommy. Tha's all he needed t' say. My boy needed me. So, here I am."

"While that was goin' on, I had a chinwag with ol' Buster. I informed him that Nell 'd be comin' with us." Da shook his head, and tossing his gaze heavenward went on, "Had t' give the man credit. Still tried to kick a bit. But when I put the squeeze on his shoulders and explained that Father Lynch was prepared t' bear witness against him about his abuse o' Nell and Tommy … well … let's just say the reality of a winter spent in the county jail settled him down."

It was then Pater's turn to speak up.

"And while these two did the dirty work, I stopped by the vicarage … sorry Father … the *rectory*. Mrs. Carlson was gracious enough to invite me in. So, I joined Tommy for a wonderful breakfast and a most illuminating conversation. Right, Tommy?"

The heat from Tommy's reddening face radiated across the table and touched everyone. A single tear escaped and ran down Tommy's cheek as he said,

"That's when mom come in with Father Lynch an' the Captain."

"Yes, and quite a scene it was, I can assure you," Pater added.

"Right, Nell?"

When I saw more than a few tears streaming down the face of this tough, downtrodden woman, I couldn't help but well-up myself. After all she'd been through, her carriage and voice still declared an unyielding dignity and grace.

Finding himself flanked by weeping females, Mr. Colgrove's face went blank. Clearly unsure of what he'd done wrong, or what to say next, he looked around the room for some cue. It was Father Lynch who offered support.

"You're doin' fine, Jeremiah, just fine."

Still unsure, Pater gave a nod and took a bracing inhalation before forging on.

"Yes, well. Nell."

"I have a problem. And I want to know if you can help me out. You see, the building we're in is called the Colgrove block. The law firm is on the first floor. CJ and Virginia live in the second floor apartment. And my son Jeremiah is moving into the third floor even as we speak. That means I own a beautiful new building filled with tenants and I have no one to run it. What do you say?"

When Nell's eyebrows furrowed and her lips pursed, Pater attempted to clarify,

"I hope you've noticed that everything about this building is new and bright. Well, I'd very much like it to stay that way. And it would, except I have these darned tenants. The law firm has clients in and out all day long; muddying the floors, filling the ashtrays, and rumpling the furniture. And as for the lawyers? Sometimes, I think all those people do all day is crumple paper and fill the trash bins."

At that, CJ and Jeremiah each crumpled a piece of paper they took from the stack on the table and tossed them at Mr. Colgrove who deftly swatted them away. When Nell quickly rose and headed off to pick up the papers, Pater resumed,

"Relax, Nell. Why not have a seat?"

"I thought you might find someone to take care of tasks such as cleaning the law offices every evening after school dismissal. Perhaps you know a young man such as that who might like to make, say, twenty five cents per week?"

Tommy perked up and was on the verge of volunteering when the phrase "after school dismissal" hit him and darkened his expression.

"As for the tenants … well, from what I hear, they're quite demanding. So, leave it to me to make sure they understand that you'll keep their pantries full, but their apartments are to be cleaned only once a week. What do you say?"

When the stunned Nell hesitated, Father Lynch stepped in,

"But won't she and Tommy be needin' a place to stay?"

"Yes, yes, Father." Pater continued. "I'd nearly forgotten. I do believe there's a vacant apartment on the fourth floor of *this* building. Might be nice and quiet up there. Would you like that, Nell?"

At that, Nell rose up and standing ramrod straight wiped left-over tears from her cheeks, and looking Pater squarely in the eye, said,

"C'mon Tommy, these people need our help. Let's get settled in an' git t' work."

Afterword

A Little Help from a Friend

No novel is created in a vacuum. In the end, its success or failure often depends upon how believable the fiction is. And since the best lies always contain elements of truth, you need to know real stuff to bolster your lies ... lots and lots of real stuff. Does that make sense?

The setting. The weather. The culture. The people. The dress. The language. The food. The tastes of the food. The smells and aromas around you. The sounds. In other words, you need go there, be there, live there. But more than that, you need to bring the reader with you.

If you're writing historical fiction, the farther back you go the harder this becomes to do. The sources you find become drier, more confusing, and less factual. Some may be so poorly written you need a translator to make sense of them. It took nearly four months of digging, reading, and dreaming to prepare writing **The Hoosac Tunnel Murders**.

Even after I began spinning the tale I hit several "Oh, oh!" moments and needed to research more.

I can't say researching ***The Textile Mill Murders*** was any more exciting. However, in digging through this sand pile I got lucky and did excavate one gem.

counting on grace (yes, the title is all lower case) is a novel written for middle school aged children or early high schoolers. However, Elizabeth Winthrop's writing style will appeal to folks of any age. The story she tells had me lost in the mills of Pownal, Vermont at a time when child labor laws may have been technically on the books but were rarely enforced.

The stacks of photos, the glossaries of terms, the textile process descriptions, the antiseptic list of job descriptions and weekly pay I was struggling to bring to life had already been molded by Ms. Winthrop into a community of people who lived them every day. In my mind's eye, the main characters weren't just Grace and Arthur. They also included a ten year-old Polish immigrant kid named Chris Wondoloski, transported in time and place to live in their world, if only for a little while. And when at the end of the story that kid returned to his sixty-eight year old reality, he shed a tear and hoped he might come close to spinning as moving a tale.

C.H.W.

Follow Mr. Wondoloski's author page on **Facebook** *at:* **Chris H. Wondoloski***, or contact him by* **email** *at:* **cwondoloski@gmail.com**

Made in the USA
Middletown, DE
10 May 2022